Left Hand

KEN MCCULLOUGH

SEISMICITY EDITIONS

A project of the Graduate Writing program
Otis College of Art & Design

LOS ANGELES ◉ 2004

Some of these pieces have appeared in the following
magazines: *Fan: A Baseball Magazine; Elysian Fields
Quarterly; 100 Words; North Coast Review; South
Dakota Review; No Exit; Poets On; Awakenings Re-
view; The Saturday Museum, River King Poetry
Supplement; The North Stone Review,* and *The New
Review of Literature.*

Book design and typesetting: Guy Bennett

SEISMICITY EDITIONS
Graduate Writing program
Otis College of Art & Design
9045 Lincoln Boulevard
Los Angeles, CA 90045

www.otis.edu
seismicity@otis.edu

For Ray DiPalma
and Dan and Bette Mongold

Table of Contents

Buffalo Nation

At White Hat's sun dance I stood talking to Daniele, my Italian friend, son of Gloria (both glorious people), and he said, as the sun set, the moon up full, that he'd like to make a documentary that did the sun dance justice. We both understood that such a film would be forbidden. I said to him, "Maybe you could get permission to just record the drumming from over here, at a distance from the arbor, and point your camera up at the clouds as backdrop." Just then, from the north, a herd of buffalo moved steadily across the sky and D and I looked at each other and roared, knowing that scenario would never recur even if the two of us were rooted there for the next one hundred sun dances; yet we'd come to expect such affirmations.

near St. Francis, S. D.
1997

The Heist

It was the summer of '65. I'd been driving a cab for four months in Newark, Delaware; except for the occasional doldrum, it was exhausting work, with no letup. If you've done it, you know that you hear and see some fairly seedy stuff, and that, next to bartenders, you learn more about people than you ever wanted to know, but that's several other stories.

Some of my fares were bookies on their way to the track; a few of them had given me tips, unsolicited (hinted at would be more accurate), but not once had they paid off. One evening the dispatcher sent me to The Deer Park, a local tavern, to pick up a fare bound for the track. My day fares went to Delaware Park, the turf races. This one was bound for Brandywine Raceway, across Wilmington, up near the Pennsylvania line. Sulky races. Turns out it was a guy I knew named George. We'd been in some plays together in college before I'd dropped out. I hadn't seen George in two years. He'd graduated and was now "looking into some options." He was just the same – a wiry little guy with darting eyes and hair that he could never keep in place. Still had the same dandruff I remembered, still smoked cork-tipped cigarillos.

"So howzit going for you, ace?" he said. I told him that this cab thing was pretty tedious but it was a living, and that I was still seeing Ruth, a chick I'd snagged from one of the plays we'd all been in together. George said to say "hi" from him.

I said, "You know, I used to be a pretty shitty driver before this job. I'd probably run a red light or a stop sign once a week – I was off there in the ozone. But having to hump it like this,

I've developed 360-degree vision at 80 miles an hour. But sometimes I don't even have time to take a piss and the dispatcher will take my order for a sandwich and throw it in the window as I drive by." I was exaggerating a little bit, but not much.

We talked about some of our mutual acquaintances, especially the foxy women and the rumors surrounding them. Most of my own exploits were strictly in my imagination, and my guess was that George probably wasn't too far ahead of me. Finally he got a little quiet and said, "How'd you like to make some quick cash, maybe get out of this cab for a spell?"

"What's up?" I said.

"Call your dispatcher and tell 'em you have to wait for your fare. I want you to come in with me and I'll show you my plan." He handed me a crisp C-note and I made my call.

We pulled in off Naaman's Road to the parking lot of Brandywine and followed the crowd in through the gates. George paid for both of us. I'd never been to a harness track before, or any kind of track, for that matter. When we came out into the grandstand, the cadence of the horses' hooves clopping on the track as they warmed up, the look of the sulkies behind the horses with their wheels spinning, the mix of smells and the variety of people all put me back into a time which otherwise no longer existed. I'd been to games in several of the old ballparks which have since been torn down, like the Polo Grounds, Griffith Stadium, and Connie Mack and this reminded me of those atmospheres – yeah, there was a sleazy element, too, but there was also something soothing about the whole thing. I asked George when they'd built this place and he said he thought in the early '50s. I'd have figured older than that – maybe it was seeing it at night.

We made our way up to the clubhouse bar. I saw another guy I knew sitting at a table by himself nursing a beer staring off into space: Joe Blahnik. He was a pretty boy from one of the blue-collar frats – looked kind of like a blond version of Joe Namath. I knew him from some of their drinking parties. Blahnik was perpetually surly but always had a looker hanging all over him. Maybe the surliness was part of his charm. He never looked at you, he looked through you. The only other time I'd ever seen that look was once when I tried to attract the attention of a caged hyena that was pacing back and forth at the zoo.

We walked up to Blahnik and George introduced us. "You two know each other?" Blahnik did his best to focus on me, but he couldn't quite do it. We acknowledged each other and shook hands. George said, "Beers?" and went to get three tall draws.

He led us down to the betting windows and said, "Joe's heard all this, but here's the basic plan: we take turns – every third race you scope out that window – the $50 window. I'll take races 1, 4 and 7; Joe, you do 2, 5 and 8 and Mac gets 3, 6 and 9. There are usually two daily doubles – they move them around. You figure out who seems to have bet a bundle, then you follow them back to where they're sitting. Then follow them again if they come back to collect. You see that woman in line? The one with the poufy hair? She's here most every night and I *know* she wins big. Harness racing in general is pretty crooked so she maybe has some kind of in…. Just before the 9th race we get together and hopefully one of us will have spotted a big winner by then. Even though there's more money in the double, it may be a moot point, Mac. We follow them out to the parking lot, tail them to a safe spot then rob them."

"You've gotta be shitting me!" I said.

"Keep your voice down. No I'm not. Nothing like this is a sure bet but I've studied this and I know its possible. Let's go outside and talk over the details."

We went down to the paddock where they were getting the horses and sulkies ready, and found a spot where we could keep an eye on things but no one would hear what we were saying. The first thing Blahnik said was, "We gotta have a gun."

"This is nuts!" I thought to myself.

"No gun," George said. I was relieved – hugely. He looked at me and said, "We're just talking about a dry run, okay?" I nodded and he continued: "After we figure out who our mark is, Mac, you will go to the car, since you're the best driver, I'll follow the mark, and Joe will position himself somewhere in between to signal you. You pick me up, then Joe, and the chase is on!"

"You really think we can keep up in traffic like that?" I said. I'd driven by when the park was letting out. I wasn't sure how many lanes there were exactly, but several.

"I guess we'll find out. As soon as we can, we'll switch drivers. Joe, you will take over, and Mac, you'll get in back with me, where we'll work on our disguises together. The next part is the part you might not like – you are bigger and stronger than I am, so when we confront the mark, if he or she resists, you'll have to deal with it." Another sinking feeling, way deep. I could feel my life going around a bend from which I could never return. But I saw where George was going: knowing that Joe might be a loose cannon, George was eliminating the possibility of him doing some serious violence. He was banking on me having a cooler head.

Joe said, "You guys should at least have some pieces of pipe or something when we really do this."

"That makes sense," George said. Would I be able to react in that kind of a situation? I had never really hit anyone in anger except on the football field. This was getting spooky.

"We better pick somebody who is real old or real weak," I said.

We went upstairs to watch a race. The drivers were positioning themselves behind the starting car. George said, "That driver in the eight hole's name is Filion, new guy from Canada." I spotted a small agile man maneuvering his rig. "He's winning everything – so the payoff on his horses might not be that hot. Watch him."

The crowd focused their attention as the horses approached the gates mounted on a white Cadillac. In almost a whisper, the announcer said, "*Heeere they come*," and, as they picked up speed and the arms of the gate were raised, "*There they goooo…*" It was twice around the half-mile track, and Filion won easily. Even I could see his skill at outfoxing his opponents. Even if it was rigged, it was convincing, and a hell of a lot of fun to watch.

George went on to explain betting – the difference between "win," "place," and "show," and that all these horses were called "standardbreds," and that there were two kinds of gaits, which he pointed out to me – horses were either "trotters," which had a diagonal gait, or "pacers," whose legs moved in tandem. Now and then a horse would break stride in a race, which usually meant that they finished out of the money. "Post position" was really important. George was talking a mile a minute (here it would be a mile in two minutes) – he really seemed to know this stuff.

"What's this about disguises?" I said.

"Okay, here's the deal. I have my make-up kit from theatre, and I copped one for you. Joe will already have on a black wig and black moustache. As we're driving we'll help each other do our make-up job. We'll darken our faces and stick on some facial hair and wigs and whatever. And we'll wear gloves, of course. It will be dark by then anyway, between 9 and 9:30. By the time we've done the deed and are on our way, they'll be looking for some black guys."

Blahnik said, "Wouldn't it be simpler just to wear ski masks?"

"Maybe…we'll see. Maybe *you* should put on a ski mask just before we make the hit."

I got to thinking about our "getaway car" – I had a gray '51 Chevy with one fender that was black – that wouldn't be too cool. "What will we use for a car?" I said.

"Joe's got a '64 Olds, dark blue, kind of neutral, and it's a runner, so we can keep up with them no matter what *they* are driving. After the hit, he'll drive us to *your* car that we'll have stashed, then we split up and he goes to hide his wheels. Then we rendezvous, probably the next day."

This was happening way too fast for me. I thought to myself, what if three black guys in an Olds get picked up for this caper? I guess that was part of George's reasoning, but I didn't like it. It was getting late. I said, "I've gotta get back to work."

"This is Wednesday. How is next Wednesday for you, Mac?"

"I work day shift next week."

"Wednesday it is. That gives us a week to work out the bugs."

I went out to my cab, exhilarated. But I was sweating profusely and my hands were shaking. I didn't smoke, but I stopped at a gas station to buy some Camels. I was on automatic pilot for the rest of my shift.

*

I was napping off a midrange hangover on Monday afternoon when I heard tapping – it was George – gave me a bit of a jolt when I opened the door – he looked like one of those double-printed images you get in the Sunday funnies when they set it up wrong – an out-of-focus miniaturized cartoon version of Harry Belafonte with a Captain Kangaroo wig.

Under streetlights, he might have passed as an extra from *Showboat*. Just to give me some ideas, just to give me some ideas. He handed me a grocery bag that contained *my* make-up kit and told me I should practice. There were also a few wigs to sort through and a fake beard. I had to keep all this stuff hidden from Len, my roommate, who was nosy, had a big mouth, and drank a lot. I would too if I had his job, which was chopping the heads off mice with a miniature guillotine in a cancer research lab. Every night, after he was ripped, he'd puff up and bellow, "Death, where is thy sting?"

Ruth, my main squeeze, kept asking me what I was thinking about. No way I was going to let her in on it. I needed some space. I begged off seeing her a couple of nights, claiming I didn't feel good, but she knew something was up. The week zipped by pretty fast.

It was Wednesday soon enough. George and Blahnik showed up at 6, I popped them each a beer, and then we headed to the track. "Everybody got their disguises? Gloves?" George said. We nodded.

Blahnik let me drive the Olds so I could get the feel of it – it was a sweet machine. We had agreed to dress in neutral clothes, and all three of us wore essentially the same thing – dark long sleeve solid color cotton shirts, black chinos and black lace-up shoes. I want to say we looked like the Beagle Boys, but I suspect it was more like the Pep Boys. I joked around in my usual smart-ass way but to tell you the truth I was scared shitless. George looked over at me – "Lighten up, ace – dry run, remember?" At the same time, he passed me a piece of lead pipe about eight inches long, while touching *his* piece of pipe to his brow in a salute. Blahnik, in his usual zombie-like state, seemed oblivious to the fact that he was left out of this part of the equation. It was a ripe night, late June, the air smelled like wet dogs.

George broke the silence: "Oh, I filched some Pennsylvania plates off a junker. We'll have to switch them the day of the deed, and Joe, remember to get them off as soon as you can after we split up. No, maybe you shouldn't bother with it until you get home. Mac, we'll figure out a place to park your short – centrally located – after we do our run-through. Not too secluded, not too busy. Maybe a side street in the 'burbs that's got steady traffic. Or better yet, a parking lot that's dimly lit. Maybe behind the Post House. Guess we should have brought it along tonight…. Whatever."

We had started early to get a prime parking spot. When we arrived, it was already starting to fill up. I found an opening three in from the end, four rows back, close to one of the exits. We got out of the Olds, locked it, and with fake bravado, George said, "Wallet, watch, testicles, spectacles," patting himself in the four respective places. Blahnik cracked a repressed Elvis sneer.

We got some racing forms and took seats at the end of a row in the grandstand whereby we could come and go easily without interference. George pointed out that the daily doubles were the 3ʳᵈ and 7ᵗʰ – "That's you, Mac, and yours truly." Blahnik asked him if he wanted a beer. George said, "Not while we're on duty. Coke for me. Cokes for all, and all for one," raising his fist. Blahnik shrugged and went off to get the Cokes.

When Blahnik returned George started in on some of the old champions – names such as Flora Temple, the "bob-tailed nag" in Stephen Foster's *Camptown Races*, and Greyhound, and Star Pointer, but his favorite seemed to be Dan Patch, a horse who was owned by a guy out in Minnesota. These were all horses from way back. He threw around terms like "claiming trotter" and "tout sheet" – I had no idea what he was talking about, but he wasn't going to let me interrupt with stupid questions. I was relieved when it was time for the first race. George vanished downstairs. Almost from the start, people were out of their seats – from the backstretch on there were five sulkies running even and it wound up in a photo finish – two horses actually finished in a dead heat. Blahnik slipped out to take his turn, and George came back just before the second race. "No real prospects," he whispered, pointing his lips to the side in my direction. "How 'bout that finish?"

I told him that it looked like some of the sulkies were pretty damn close to each other, like the chariots in *Ben Hur*. "Yup, there *are* accidents now and then…. I saw a race where a guy was in a collision and had his eye gouged out…but he came back the next season to race." I've never been much of an ambulance chaser, and hoped that we'd get through the evening without something like that happening. Filion took the second race wire to wire and I excused myself.

I took a spot near the $50 window and right away spotted an old guy in a slouch hat, wearing rumpled khakis. He had a pleasantly wrinkled face. He took out a roll of bills about as big around as a hot dog bun and peeled off what looked like four or five, I couldn't tell exactly. I followed him back to where he was sitting. He was with two young guys, maybe in their late 20s. He seemed to know them pretty well. The race started and he sat there, unimpressed, while everyone else was yelling. After it was over, he went to the pay window and collected quite a bit of money.

I went back upstairs and said to Blahnik, "A definite maybe." The fourth race was uneventful, but in the fifth, Filion, who was, according to George, "parked out for a mile and a quarter," came on to win by a whisker. George was talking about the horses at this track – This Hanover, That Hanover, Hanover-ad nauseum. My turn again.

Downstairs it was déjà vu – the same old man making the

same kind of bet. I followed him down to the paddock where he talked with some of the drivers and other people (trainers, was my guess). He talked quietly and they all seemed to know him and treat him with deference. The hairs on my neck were standing up. He went back to the same seat. And then back to the pay window.

I went back to *my* seat. Blahnik had nothing to tell me. I got a hot dog, and when George returned after the 7th, I said, "I think I have our man." He gave me the thumbs up. I described the old man and George said he'd seen him many times before.

Blahnik came back empty-handed in the 8th and we decided to skip the 9th. As planned, it would be George's job to stick close to our man, while I drove and Blahnik acted as semaphore traffic director. I showed George where the old guy was sitting and we waited until he rose to leave after the 9th. He shook hands with one of the young guys while the other one followed him up the stairs. We got in the flow behind them and as soon as they were outside I sprinted for the car. It was a madhouse.

Hopefully we'd lose them and that would be the end of it. I stood outside the car with the engine running. Then I saw Blahnik frantically waving – then he and George sprinting along together. By the time they got to me they were just ahead of the Pontiac Chieftain driven by the younger man with the old guy riding shotgun. George and Blahnik hopped in, wild-eyed. I horned into the line two cars behind the Pontiac.

The traffic was horrendous and I had to cut off two lanes to stay with our man, or men. They pulled off almost immediately at the Tally-Ho Bar, at the corner of the Concord Pike and Naaman's Road. George directed me to a space in shadow. He said, "This is one of the track bars – some pretty unsavory people come in here. The other place is Stanley's, over on Faulk Road – higher class crowd…. Okay, Joe, you go in and keep an eye. We'll do this make-up thing." This would be tricky – there was still quite a bit of light, and anyone who walked by would see two men putting on make-up – that might raise a few eyebrows, and would certainly catch their eye. And if we had to wait for long, two black guys in the back seat of a car doing nothing – pretty suspicious.

Blahnik slipped on his wig, George checked it, then stuck a regimental moustache on Blahnik's upper lip. Blahnik got out and sauntered toward the bar while we got to work, applying the make-up, sticking on eyebrows and facial hair, all the while trying to have it be convincing. We worked fast – George really had this down – and checked each other as we went. We dusted with dark powder. George was done in less than two minutes; I made it in about three. We smelled like a couple of cheap hookers.

Now we had time to kill. We knew that Blahnik was drinking beer inside the Tally Ho – hopefully not too much. We pretended to be reading our racing forms in case someone passed by. A few people did, but we avoided eye contact. George had on sunglasses anyway, and I could see him scoping out the people who got into a nearby car and left.

After a lull, George said, "This intersection is the crosshairs of northern Delaware: Concord Pike is the demarcation line between the middle class and the rich – the suburbs over here to the east and to the west it's chateau country, out toward Granogue and Chadd's Ford – the Wyeths, and all that." He said this with noticeable disdain. "The Kennett Pike is the western border, then it's back to normal folks again." I'd been to the Chadd's Ford Inn twice, once on a Homecoming date I couldn't afford, and another time with some buddies when we dressed up and sat at the bar pretending to be preppies. I'd won five bucks that night off one of my comrades, identifying the object over the bar as a narwhal tusk. I understood where George was coming from – we both felt more at home in a townie bar, as long as there was room for a few oddballs.

This was taking forever. Finally our mark emerged, accompanied by the younger guy, followed at a distance by Blahnik, trying to look inconspicuous but failing. He got into the driver's seat, fired her up and we began tailing them again. Again, it wasn't easy but Blahnik was doing a decent job of it. We headed west a little, then cut back south into a suburb of older brick houses – didn't catch any street names – I was distracted, to say the least. The car came to a stop in front of a substantial but rundown brick house. We had been following at a respectable distance and had time to stop three houses down and kill our lights. "Ski mask, ski mask," George whispered to Blahnik, who complied. Our view was partially obscured by a tree, but we saw the younger man get out and go around to open the door for the old guy. They talked for about a minute and we could hear them both chuckle. They shook hands and the old man shambled toward the front door. There were no lights on in the house and just a dim outside light. The old man was illuminated by the headlights of his friend's car. He fumbled for his key in his pants pocket, and I could see the bulge of the roll of bills in his other pants pocket as he turned to wave at the other guy pulling out of the driveway.

"Let's do him now!" Blahnik said. At that moment I had visions of what would happen. George and I would rush the old man, ask for the money calmly, he would resist, yell for help, and I would have to clock him with the pipe. He was a big man, but old and out of shape. No telling how strong he was. He would struggle even though blood would be streaming from his head. George would kick him in the groin and he would go down, then we'd wrestle him for the money and I'd have to whack him again. He would lie there motionless as a neighbor's light came on and we ran for the car.

"No!" George said. "This is strictly practice." My heart rate settled down to about 200 beats a minute. We waited until the old man was inside and had switched his lights on, then we left. It appeared that he lived alone. At that moment I was glad it hadn't happened – the old guy had kind of grown on me. And I knew he wouldn't be that lucky next time.

George and I worked furiously at getting the make-up and stuff off while Blahnik drove. It took us a while – then we smelled like cold cream. Maybe we'd have to rethink this part of the plan. George said, "Let's go back toward Concord Pike and find a good place to park the other car."

Blahnik said, "We should have done it right then…everything was perfect."

And I could have killed a man over what? Maybe a thousand bucks, or less? George just waved Blahnik off. We got back onto Concord Pike, turned at Naaman's and went a ways before we turned off again and cruised, looking. We settled on Amnesty Drive. Blahnik was still brooding.

Given the fact that George and I still showed traces of make-up, we decided to stop at a package store and grab a six-pack of Schmidt's rather than go to a bar. We just sat in the car, hashed over the evening, and agreed that everything had gone smoothly, that this was indeed do-able. George still wanted to do the make-up thing, but Blahnik said, "Bullshit, man – that's pointless – go with ski masks or stockings." I didn't say anything but that made sense to me. George said, "Okay, men, we'll stay in touch on this, and set the date as soon as we can. Next week, or the week after at the latest."

The two of them dropped me off. Len, who had a pretty good buzz on, gave me the fish eye, but went back to his book.

I cleaned up all traces and then hit the sack: work tomorrow bright and early.

Two days later I got a call from George: Blahnik had received his draft notice and had to report for his physical immediately. Our plan would be on hold until his situation became clear. Well, about two weeks later George finally called back – Joe was 1-A: we'd have to find a new third man. I knew, at that moment, that we'd never go through with it. I took a union laborer's job in Chicago at the end of the summer and that was that.

I never went to Brandywine again, never saw another harness race. I hear that there's a huge shopping mall where Brandywine used to be. Roosevelt Park, in New York, which used to average 20,000 a night, was down to about 4,000 by the late '80s, and they closed just before Brandywine. Liberty Bell, in Philly, gone too. Replaced by the likes of The Meadowlands and Dover Downs. But Concord Pike still divides the Haves from the Wanna-Haves.

Ballad of a Thin Man

We pulled off I-25 into an Amoco at the Starkville exit to gas up. Just below Trinidad, north of the New Mexico border. We'd been on the road from Wisconsin for two days. Slow going – a gas-hog Chrysler pulling a U-Haul loaded with carefully-wrapped incriminating chemicals. We were moving the makings of an acid lab to Oakland. Supposed to be there by the evening of December 7th. Things had gotten so complicated back in Wisconsin that our backers had decided to cut bait and relocate the base of operations. Our local boss was a guy our age, whom all of us had known for a couple of years, and was paying us a decent wage. He had bought a house outside Argyle, far enough from Madison not to attract attention with comings and goings, and had converted the basement into a hidden lab – had two carpenters in his employ who'd bricked in the basement entrance, fashioned a well-concealed escape route, and put in some vents. The carpenters had cut a trap door into the living room floor that was hidden by a rug – that was the main way in. The intention of the backers was to create a product that aficionados would regard as reliable and pure.

The local contact, let's call him Lester, had a grad student in Chemistry, Laxton, who ordered the chemicals through university channels. I was "renting" the farmhouse where I was supposedly "working on a novel" – that was our cover. The bosses had hired two acid chemists from the Bay Area, trained by Owsley, who had flown in separately to check out the facility. More on them later. Everybody was extra-careful – a lot of cloak-and-dagger stuff. But then they started getting paranoid – there was a small plane that kept flying over, ostensibly checking the nearby power-lines; there was a guy in an old MG with one headlight out who kept showing up in rearview mirrors, etc. That's when they made the decision to move west.

We had even started to suspect each other, which was par for the course in those days, when every other person was an FBI informant. Just before they decided to close up shop, they even had me sneak up to the farmhouse, driving with my lights out, crawl through a cornfield, and drag out two big bottles of lysergic acid, the most obvious chemical we had on the shelves. I was directed to take the bottles to a spot known only to me and bury them until further notice. I drove them to an abandoned barn near a house I'd once rented and buried them, deep. All the while stopping every mile or so to wait for anyone who might be following, and getting out of the car to see if there was a plane up there without running lights. Maybe they had planted a homing device on my car. You get the idea. Zim, one of the carpenters, told me that Todd, the other carpenter, who spoke in the measured monotone of someone who'd taken downers over a long period of time, had it worked out that if anything happened to him, he had it fixed that everyone else involved in this operation would "get waxed." I didn't ask for corroboration.

It was decided that Laxton, the chemist, and I would ferry the chemicals to the Coast using Laxton's Chrysler. Before we left, Lester had said, "If you guys get popped, we'll have you out in no time. We'll get you out of the country, with enough money to live in style for the rest of your lives.... Questions?"

Hell, yes, I had questions. The rest of my life in exile, not being able to see my family, not being able to go to another major league game? Where was Lester going to come up with that kind of bread? But I said nothing. Nor did Laxton.

I mulled over what I knew about Lester, most of it hearsay. Lester was connected; his family lived out on the north shore of Long Island and had cooked the books for the mob. He'd graduated first in his class at Exeter, then at Harvard. They had brought him to Madison as the next economics whiz. He also played piano, both jazz and classical, and it was rumored that he'd ghosted some songs for Leonard Cohen. But he was a slave to his appetites. He ingested and injected every drug known to man, the stronger the better. His pattern with women was that they all fell for him and tried to fly with him until their wings gave out. Lester liked to gamble on anything; he made lots of money instantaneously then blew it just as quickly. He was starting to develop some eccentricities not unlike Howard Hughes; for instance, when he got a room in a motel it had to be on the top floor and he took the rooms on either side also so that he had privacy. At hotels, he'd order everything on the room service breakfast menu so that he didn't have to decide.

I'd met Lester in the bars, which Lester didn't frequent that often, but when he did he was always the center of attention, doing a non-stop stand-up routine. He'd finished his coursework and left town. I saw him again a year later, on the street in Madison one Sunday morning. We'd made small talk, and then Lester had asked me how it was going. I'd told him that I was running a rock drill down at the bottom of a caisson ten hours a day and that even though I wore a mask, the dust was starting to kill me, as well as the sensory deprivation of being down in a tube for that length of time. Lester had gotten a sympathetic look on his face, and then he asked me what my debts were at the time. I'd calculated quickly in my head – about 1,100 bucks. Lester had taken out his wallet and removed eleven new hundred-dollar bills and handed them to me. He put his arm on my shoulder and said, "There's a lot more where this came from."

I was in my bar-of-choice that night, and a guy I knew, a big loudmouth named Gary, was bragging about all the money he'd made as a dealer in Tahoe. We were standing next to the pool table. I opened my wallet and took out the hundreds, displaying them like a winning hand: "I've been doing okay, myself." Gary's eyes got big and it actually caused him to miss a beat – a rarity.

Unlike Lester, I didn't have much use for dope. I didn't mind a toke now and then, and often became a voluble raconteur afterwards, and I certainly enjoyed the way it changed the way things looked. But more often than not, when I smoked around other people, which was par for the course, I became paranoid. On one occasion I showed up at a party, smoked, and within minutes noticed that everyone there was speaking an elaborate kind of code, and I was the object of their plot. The greatest espionage writers in the world could not have written a more intricate script.

I'd taken LSD only twice, and both times nothing had happened. The first time was of no consequence, but the other, my friend Ramona had arrived from the East Coast with several hits of blotter acid that had been manufactured in a lab – pure stuff. We'd dropped together out at my shack on the river. Very soon Ramona was down at the river wading around in a trance. I, on the other hand, felt nothing, so I took another 900 mics, knowing I might become one of those cases you hear about who wind up around the bend and never come back. But even then nothing happened. Finally I smoked some hash with two buddies who had shown up and regaled them with tall tales. Ramona was still tripping into the evening hours. The next day she had said, "Maybe you are so afraid of letting go that you're blocking the effects." Could be. I didn't have a better answer.

All the other guys involved in this scheme were users and believers. Except for Laxton who believed only in German beer and expensive single malt Scotch. Part of me thought that it was hypocritical that I myself, who was not a believer, was part of this. Laxton was in it for the thrill, obviously. Why was *I* doing it? For the money?

Laxton had procured all the chemicals through legitimate requisition forms – it looked good on paper – he was slick all right. He was doing research, didn't have to teach, so he could take off any time he wanted – no one would be suspicious. Well, yes, all of us were paranoid at this point, but I had a particular distrust of Laxton; sure that if it came down to it, Laxton would waste me before you could say Mrs. Robinson. Laxton featured himself as the reincarnation of Ernest Hemingway. He had his mustache trimmed the same way, the same arrogant demeanor. And the same fascination with firearms: he had cut into the door panel on the driver's side of the Chrysler and made a compartment with a Velcro flap where he kept a Walther P38. He also carried a smaller-caliber pistol in a well-concealed shoulder holster. For all I knew, Laxton had other guns at hand – I didn't want to know. Laxton was a prick of the first order, but it had been apparent to me that I wouldn't have much of a payday unless I accompanied Laxton on this trip. He would have made a good Nazi officer.

Yes, it was slow going in the Chrysler. Most of our small talk was about guns, cars, those things important to most males with any cojones. The Chrysler was a guzzler, and pulling that trailer meant we were getting single digits in terms of miles per gallon. Lester had given us gas money, but the way we had it figured, after two days we might run through all of it and most of our own cash.

There were a few snowflakes swirling in the air and it was getting nippy as Laxton topped it off and we pulled back on the entrance to the Interstate. The heater in the Chrysler was kind of uneven, so our visibility was impaired, and before we realized it we were on the narrow frontage road, snow piled high on both sides, room for just one car. We decided to turn around the first chance we got, but that chance wasn't forthcoming. After about a mile, we saw a neon sign, "Nico's Place," with a split rail fence surrounding the parking lot, making it look like a corral.

Laxton said, "Shit, let's get out of here!" and started to maneuver the car and trailer through the turnaround. Unfortunately, the wheels of the trailer went off into the ditch – we couldn't get any traction – we were stuck. "Get out and jump on the bumper of the trailer," Laxton said. I did this, but it didn't help. Just as I got back in, six guys in cowboy hats piled out of the bar and moseyed in our direction. Laxton popped the Velcro to his hidden compartment – I saw that he had his hand on the Walther P38. I'd just seen *Easy Rider* – the ending of that movie was the image that came to my mind.

One cowboy tapped on the window. Laxton slid the pistol back into the pocket and rolled down the window.

"Stuck, eh? We'll push you out, and if we can't, Nico has a winch on his truck."

I got out to help them. They were all drunk and at one point one of them actually fell under the trailer's spinning rear tire – he just laughed it off with the rest of them. I noticed that said cowboy seemed a little more flamboyant than the others.

Finally they rocked her out of the ditch – we were high and dry. The spokesman of the group said, "You come inside and we'll buy you a drink!" Laxton and I looked at each other – two against the world. Wouldn't be polite, though, to refuse their Western Hospitality. As we walked toward the bar, all I could think of was the ending of another movie – *Butch Cassidy and the Sundance Kid* – where they emerge into the sunlight to be cut down in slow motion by the Federales.

We entered the front door, everyone in high spirits. Nico's was an ordinary-looking bar. It was Friday night – a decent crowd. The spokesman introduced himself as Dean (of course), and said that a group called Freezing Point was coming in to play around 9, and that they were pretty hot. I could see that Laxton was still wound pretty tight.

Just then a dark trim little guy in a beige Ban-lon shirt with the top button buttoned came in from the kitchen. "I'm Nico, short for Domenikos – Greek. Have whatever you want, on the house. Glad these guys could get you out…. Where you boys headed?"

Laxton told him Santa Fe, then 'Frisco. I recognized Jean Shepard and Ferlin Huskey singing "Dear John" on the jukebox – hadn't heard that tune since the '50s.

I ordered a double shot of Wild Turkey and a tall draft. All of us kept drinking and by now we were starting to swap stories. Laxton was loosening up. The flamboyant guy was quite attentive. Nico had ducked back into the kitchen. Then Laxton got very quiet all of a sudden and his face got ashen. He motioned that he was going outside, "I'll be right back, guys."

I realized what was up: what if some of those damn bottles had broken while they were bouncing and lurching around? – we'd be in deep shit. I got a little quiet myself. Laxton returned a long three minutes later and gave the high sign – no damage. He had big snowflakes on his coat. Just then a couple came in and said, "Pretty bad going over the pass." They were referring to Raton Pass – where we were headed.

Nico returned. "I'd like you two to come with me." By now we'd both been drinking those double shots and beers and had lowered our defenses – the place seemed benign enough, so we followed him through the kitchen into an area which was called a "conversation pit" in those days – sunken, like a kiva, with three tiers in a kind of amphitheater arrangement. There was a gas fire going in the center of the pit. And a passageway around the top of the pit, with rooms radiating like the spokes of a wheel, each room in a different color – dark rose, cerulean blue, butterscotch, lime green, a kind of paisley design, burnt orange, and, believe it or not, zebra stripes.

Nico said, "There are more rooms down that hallway. I have another operation outside of Walsenberg, but I should have this one up and running by mid-January. I'll get most of my girls from Denver – $50 tricks, but we'll upgrade them here. I expect to draw from Albuquerque, Phoenix, Denver, maybe even Dallas." He motioned us back through the door to the kitchen. More couples were coming in, anticipating the music. All of them covered in snowflakes. I looked out the door – it was really coming down.

Nico said, "I wouldn't try the pass tonight. Could be dangerous…. I'll call two of my girls from Walsenberg and set you up – my treat. Should let up by morning." Laxton and I had both thrown down a fair amount of booze by then, and our bravado meter was starting to climb. And everything we said and did fascinated or titillated the flamboyant cowboy, Richie.

I said to Laxton, "We're supposed to be in Oakland by the tomorrow night – they'll all be there. If we come in late that may throw a monkey wrench into their schedule."

"Yeah, we'd better head out," said Laxton.

I wondered what the women from Walsenberg were like –

Playboy bunnies, or high plains heifers? – I was tempted but intimidated at the same time.

Nico overheard us: "You're making a big mistake, but, hey, it's your call."

Richie was looking particularly at Laxton when he said, "I think you should definitely stay."

But we were resolved – the booze had given us a false sense of our own abilities – we were going to shove off. We said our good-byes and thanks, there was some backslapping and someone said, "Come back any time." This seemed to be unanimous. Nico shook hands with us and said, "You have to promise me that you'll stop the next time you pass through, to check on business." He winked. We agreed, thanked him and were out the door into the Bing Crosby snow.

Big wet snow, and I noted that it was indeed piling up and starting to drift across the road as we pulled away from Nico's with our buddies hanging out the door, waving. It was blowing pretty hard. When we got back onto the Interstate we were hit by a swirling tailwind countered by the steep grade and the slick surface. We poked along. The only traffic coming down Raton Pass from the other direction was a big snow-plow and a tow truck hauling a van. The Chrysler didn't have 4-wheel drive – not many cars did in those days – and Laxton didn't have chains. I flipped on the overhead light but there was nothing on the map indicating how far it was to the top of the pass. We were getting nowhere.

Eventually we had zero traction, literally. Laxton said, "Why don't you get out and jump on the trailer bumper?" I don't know why I agreed to do it, but I opened the door to get out – the wind was terrific; I had a hard time wrestling the door shut. I was out there jumping up and down for several minutes and had burned off much of the alcohol I'd consumed. I felt like I was barely conscious. No traffic at all now.

When I gave up and returned to the car the wind almost ripped off the door when I opened it. Laxton said, "I'm not sure how much more of this I can take…. There's no way of knowing whether a tow truck will ever come by…and it will cost a mint – we won't have enough left for gas."

I wanted to say, "You shitbird! You've just been sitting here on your ass – what the hell's your problem, you arrogant fucking asshole?" But I didn't say it. Instead, I said, "Let's open both the front doors. I think we might get just enough boost from the wind to get us moving."

Laxton shrugged his shoulders and pushed open his door, with great effort. I did the same, and got out to add my weight to the trailer once again. I was wearing a watch cap, but the wind was cutting right through it. Sure as shit, we started creeping up Raton Pass at about five miles an hour. The wind was numbing my entire head, but I stayed out there until we reached the top. An eternity. I got back in and we took turns closing our doors, which had to be done quickly because now we ran the risk of getting too much momentum going down the other side.

I needed to thaw out. Laxton said, "I can't do this anymore." No point arguing with him. Laxton put on the emergency brake and we switched places. I started gingerly down Raton Pass into New Mexico, the full trailer making its presence felt behind us. I thought of those old mail planes (DeHavilands?) with the gas tanks in the rear and what happened to the pilots when they crashed. The wind had shifted and the snow was coming at us like a blinding meteor shower.

After ten or fifteen minutes of absolute concentration on the road in front of me, I saw a large baby lying across the road. It was a least ten feet long, probably longer. I knew it didn't really exist, but there it was anyway. I braced myself and plowed through the apparition. Then I shook Laxton awake and told him we were pulling over at the first turn-out and I was going to sleep, with the engine running. "If we are asphyxiated, so be it."

We woke at false dawn, very hung over, and continued down the pass and on to Santa Fe where we crashed at a motel for about four hours. I'd never been down there before. There was a beautiful dusting of snow on the red pockmarked hills leading into and around Santa Fe. The air smelled better than air anywhere else.

Coffee and some huevos rancheros and we were on our way again. We swung west on 40, the old Route 66 – we were like an updated counter-culture episode of the TV show, with a bomb of a Chrysler instead of a new Corvette. Some people had even told me that I resembled the George Maharis character, Buzz Murdock – the same dark good looks. I kept the analogy to myself, knowing that if I brought it up, Laxton would appropriate Murdock and I'd be stuck in the bland Martin Milner role.

Laxton played mostly rockabilly stations, which was okay with me. We gassed at Laguna Pueblo. In the store, a knock-out in her teens gave me "the look" – oh, that we'd had time. Farther west, we drove into Gallup. I remember saying, "If Dante had been an American Indian he would have dreamed up this place." And before we hit the border to California, Laxton had wrapped and stashed all his weapons in a compartment under the Chrysler. He'd also gotten out his inventory and a phony letter on UC-Berkeley Chem Department letterhead that validated his existence. I saw the list: sodium acetate, lithium aluminum hydride, ammonia, lysergic acid, ether, acetonitrile, ethanol, thionyl chloride, ethyl amine, dry nitrogen, etc. – apparently most of it pretty innocent except for lysergic acid, lithium aluminum hydride and thionyl chloride. We talked about what would happen if the trailer were searched, and Lester's words came to mind: "We'll have you out in no time." But the guy at the agricultural checkpoint just asked a few questions then had us open the doors to the trailer. He gave it the once over and said we were okay. Didn't even look at the documents.

Through Needles and the middle of the Mojave Desert, the Joshua trees along the ridges like the silhouettes of grotesque prospectors. Past Edwards AFB where Chuck Yaeger and his cronies did their test flight thing. Through Barstow and onto 58 now. Somewhere around Boron I was starting to fade – off to the right, I caught a glimpse of a large factory covered in white dust – maybe the 20 Mule Team Borax plant. Laxton woke me at Bakersfield as we turned north on to 99.

"Merle Haggard country," he said. My turn to drive. I recalled also that Kerouac had spent a few idyllic weeks down this way in a town called Sabinel, picking grapes, living with a young Mexican woman and her kid.

Near Tulare, I saw a Lincoln Continental stopped in the middle of the highway and pulled over to investigate. "What are you doing, man? We need to make time." But I sprinted broken-field out to the car, which looked as if it had been sand-blasted. The woman in the front seat was yelling to no one in particular. She was fairly young, wearing good clothes, but reeked of booze and piss. Alcohol had already etched her face. Her skirt was hiked up and she wasn't wearing underpants.

She focused her sunken eyes on me and said defiantly, "What the fuck do *you* want?"

I signaled for Laxton to come over then reached in and shifted her car into neutral, the two of us pushed it off onto the shoulder with me steering as best I could, amidst the blaring traffic. We beat it before the cops could come along and misinterpret anything. As we drove away, I could still hear the woman ranting.

Tulare – home of Bob Mathias, two-time Olympic decathlon champion, now a u.s. Senator. As a kid, I'd seen the movie about Mathias's life and was sure my own life would turn out the same way. Probably most kids who saw the movie thought the same thing. Every time a Highway Patrol car passed, I got a queasy feeling.

At Manteca I veered west on 205, and picked up 580, which would take us in to Oakland. In the yellow-brown hills near Livermore, we passed through what looked like the aftermath of a battle minus the bomb craters: hundreds of lost-looking hippies wandering around, trash everywhere, junked-out campsites, people trying to start their hopeless vehicles, even the burned-out shell of a van. We had no idea what this was all about until we talked to Lester in Oakland: it was December 7th, the day before had been the free Rolling Stones concert at the Altamont Raceway – 850 people injured, two run over in their sleeping bags, another drowned. The Stones' bodyguards, the San Francisco Hell's Angels, had bludgeoned a young black man named Meredith Hunter to death with leaded pool cues while Jagger strutted through "Under My Thumb."

We found our rendezvous point easily – the Denny's near the Oakland Coliseum. I pulled in to the parking lot and maneuvered into truck parking. The guy we were meeting, Sid, was the mastermind of this whole operation – Lester's buddy from his Harvard days. In fact, all the partners in this entrepreneurial venture had been buddies at Harvard – all geniuses, from Lester's sketchy descriptions of them, and all, just like Lester, a bit out of control.

The only time I'd laid eyes on Sid, he'd flown in from the Coast to check out the lab. Came roaring up with Lester to where Todd and I were tinkering with Todd's old t-Bird. Lester and Sid jumped out and scurried into the house as if someone were hot on their tails. It was October, Indian Summer, but Sid was wearing a ski mask, which he kept on throughout his visit – so that we would not be able to identify him. He had hyper-alert blue eyes. I would know those eyes anywhere. After two minutes in his presence, it was clear to me that Sid was a risk junkie.

And speaking of disguises, not long after that I was told to meet one of the acid chemists at the airport. A football weekend, Badgers everywhere, in red and white outfits. I spotted a ferret-faced guy in a long leather coat, wearing an obvious wig, walked up and tapped him on the shoulder. The guy ("Karl with a K") wheeled around and was in my face: "How'd you know it was me?"

"Just a guess, I guess," I said. We picked up Karl's luggage – a brand new K-Mart trunk. I'd thought to myself "Trunk, wig, long leather coat – now you tell *me*." Karl made his inspection and I took him back to the airport the next day. He left the trunk. Another chemist appeared and left a week later in a similar manner.

Anyway, we went into Denny's, got a booth and waited.

"What do you know about this Sid?" said Laxton.

"That he and Lester were classmates at Harvard and that he changes residences and phone numbers every three – you heard me – three days and never uses the same name. And that he's addicted to exotic cars."

Pretty soon a Ferrari barrel-assed into the parking lot, and a guy in a leather coat and Afro got out and strode in the front door. I motioned him over. Intense blue eyes, worried look: "How did you know it was me?"

"Just a guess," I said. Laxton and I exchanged glances.

We were five minutes into our conversation when six strapping cops walked in – four occupied the booth on one side of us desperados, the other two the booth on the other side – "a cop sandwich," I thought. I could see Sid's blue eyes get wider, a catch in his voice. In actuality, what had happened was that the Raiders game had ended and the cops, who had been directing the traffic exiting the Coliseum, had just completed their shift. Lester showed up and we all had a good laugh about it, at Sid's expense.

Lester directed us to a warehouse, where we dropped the trailer. Then we followed him to the motel where we'd stay the night and the meet with the other partners would take place.

I called up my old girlfriend from Madison, Janice, who was in San Francisco trying to make it as a commercial artist. I told her I was out there "taking care of some business," but that I'd be free, probably, by tomorrow evening – asked could we get together, and if it was possible for me to crash at her place. She was usually upbeat, but sounded genuinely pleased that I had called. As I hung up I relapsed into the loss I'd felt when we'd split up. She could give no reason – she loved me, she'd said, but the fit wasn't right – she was confused, about everything; I was confused; Madison was coming apart at the seams. Who knows why I was sniffing around her again. Wishful thinking probably. Janice had a lot of class and she always lit up a room – I had no hard feelings – she'd always been decent to me.

We cleaned up, ate some decent food in Chinatown – red lacquered booths in a walk-down restaurant, and got back in time for the meet – the Ivy League geniuses and their foot soldiers, Laxton and I, two chemists. The third partner, Howie, had just gotten back from a big acid conference in Switzerland and the news was mixed – he should hear from his contacts in the wee hours, then they'd know their next move. Lester and his two chums looked and acted like overgrown kids, but all three were, indeed, complex dynamos – you could hear the gears spinning.

They broke out some beers and Lester started joking around about the paranoia that had been going around. I'm not sure what possessed me, maybe I thought it would get me points, but I said off-handedly, "Yeah, Todd even had it worked out that the rest of us would go down if he took a fall…. Can you believe that?" There was stone cold silence. They all looked at me. Lester had a sickened expression that said, "Don't you have any goddamn sense?" The conversation picked up again and after 45 minutes Lester said he needed to split and that he'd see us at "0900 hours sharp."

The next morning we had the privilege of shopping with Lester and Howie for (what else?) Italian leather coats. Lester took us aside and said that he had bad news – "The bottom's fallen out of the acid market – so we're not even going to begin out here. I'll pay you for this trip and next month, but I'm afraid that's it."

"That's it?" I thought. "Four months of solitary confinement, to barely break even?" Was this about my remark last night? They'd decided I was a liability? They'd fabricated this reason just to cut me out of the action?

I'd had visions (or were they delusions?) of a nest egg. I knew a guy who'd been a dealer for a few years and now owned a fancy bar in Morocco – he came back to Madison once a year – you'd see him scanning the financial news over his morning coffee.

When I had become involved in this back in late August I was shacked up with a woman I really dug. In fact I had wanted to marry her. But she was into free love and alternative everything, although she still wanted me around. When I had moved to the house outside Argyle the deal was I was supposed to stay there, tell no one of my whereabouts or activities, and make no personal phone calls from the house. My woman, Anna, had moved into a house with two other women, and when I did call her it was from a phone booth at a road-side diner. I knew this could be traced, of course. I was able to make these calls free of charge because Paul Newman had published his credit card number in the *L.A. Free Press*, or someone had. This worked until one day there was an un-usually long silence when I gave the operator the credit card number – the jig was up – back to using my own dime. It was tough maintaining a tenuous relationship long-distance, par-ticularly with a tenuous person in tenuous times.

Anna and I had met secretly on several occasions and be-ing around her, knowing that she'd been sleeping with other guys, just made me want her all the more. I was like a hound dog in rut. She was hot, and I couldn't stay away. We'd drive around the countryside looking at abandoned farmhouses, taking a meal at some small-town diner, or go into a movie separately and move together partway through, or make love in the soft grass out behind a neglected country cemetery. But I digress.

The four of us, Howie, Lester, Laxton, and I, continued the search for the ideal leather coat. We finally wound up in an outrageously expensive shop, mahogany and brass, where a florid salesman was waiting on a couple. He swished and swooped around the man, who was in his 40s and had the tall, rugged good looks of a typical Australian, patting as he went. The woman was cute and bland – American, and in her early 20s. The couple wound up with mirrored vests from Afghani-stan and coats with shaggy sheepskin linings. I checked the prices on the racks – a run-of-the-mill leather vest for $400. I stopped listening to the salesman's patter and just watched the shameless fawning. When their transaction was complete, the salesman turned his attention to Howie. Four attractive young men – what a chance to perform! And it was quite a show – Howie loved every minute of it and brought the level of innuendo up several notches. Mission accomplished: he and Lester both walked out with black leather coats soft as babies' butts.

It was getting dark, a chill in the air, rain on the way. Lester paid us our pittance and we were on our own – "no direction home/like a rolling stone," I thought to myself. Laxton said he'd give me a ride to Janice's apartment. On the way, he asked if he could tag along – he had nothing to do, nowhere to go: "Do you think I could crash there, too? …And maybe we'll split some time tomorrow."

By this time I'd developed a full-fledged allergy to the tone of Laxton's voice. But I said, "Yeah, okay," figuring I had to maintain some semblance of civility if we were going to make the return trip without a blow-up – and I couldn't afford to waste money on a flight. Maybe we'd stop at Nico's.

Janice lived just on the edge of Haight-Ashbury, on Stanyan. We cruised around to look over the Haight – neither of us had ever been there before. Things were a mess – flower power must have been on the wane. The people on the street looked mean, like smack freaks, each with a German shepherd in tow. There were piles of dogshit all over the sidewalks. Roger Miller was singing a song on the radio called "Me and Bobby McGee" – "Freedom's just another word for nothin' left to lose" – You said it, brother. A good song, but kind of raw for Roger Miller. The deejay said it was written by a young guy named Kristofferson, whose songs were making the rounds. It would be good to see Janice – part of our relationship had been stuck in the Johnny Mathis aspect of the button-down '50s – maybe we'd both outgrown that by now.

We found her place, parked on the street, and she buzzed us in. Third floor walk-up, steep stairs and lots of intricate woodwork. Her long blonde hair was up in a bun, her figure was great as usual, and so was her toothy smile. I introduced Laxton and asked if it would be okay if he crashed there. She said why not, he could have the couch. She kissed me long and deep and took my knapsack and threw it in on her bed. Nice place. She'd been there only a year, but she'd filled it with eccentric furniture and many of her own paintings and drawings lined the walls. One, a nude I had posed for. That gave me a bit of a rise.

She got us a couple of Anchor Steams – a local brew, bold and hoppy. Laxton struck his most knowledgeable pose and began comparing the beer with others he'd had. For him, everything was competition, and he was doing his best to impress Janice – and damned if it wasn't working; they were developing a lively repartee, name-dropping a mile-a-minute. She suggested we go to a good Russian restaurant nearby. She'd throw on a dress and we should spiff up in whatever way we could. Laxton had a safari jacket in his knapsack – in keeping with his Hemingway image. All I had was a burgundy-colored peasant shirt Howie had bought me that afternoon. I noticed Laxton give Janice's backside a hungry look as she passed by to the bedroom.

The restaurant was the real deal: run by white Russians, the waiter and maître d' were Russian, and there was a Russian violinist accompanying a large round man who sang Russian gypsy songs in a mellow bass. The furnishings were exquisite and the menu, of course, was in Russian. When we entered the singer immediately greeted us with "Lara's Theme" from *Dr. Zhivago*.

Laxton knew a little Russian, of course. And he did his best to contradict and undermine everything I said. He made astute suggestions about the menu and choice of wines. Janice was developing a glow when she talked with him, and they were starting to leave me out on the periphery. I, in turn, was getting surly. Laxton called over the waiter: "More beluga, *bojaluysta*." The bill was going to be horrendous, of course. Just as we finished our entrées, the singer directed a song in our direction – "for my friends." He said the title, *"Ochi Chyornie,"* and then began singing:

> *Ochi Chyornie*
> *Ochi Strastnie*
> *I prekrasnie*
> > *Kak lyublyu ya vas*
> > *Kak boyusi ya vas*
> > *Znat' uridel vas*
> > *Ya ne v dobriy chas....*

His delivery was dramatic, and the content of the song was clearly romantic, possibly even tragic. The violin fluttered mournfully. None of us knew what the words meant, but Janice was blushing – I got the distinct feeling that both she and Laxton thought that the singer and violinist were playing their song.

After dessert we took a short constitutional, but it was starting to rain, so we returned to her place. Going up the stairs Laxton cut me off and fell in behind Janice, following closely.

Janice lit up a joint, which was her wont – I was starting to get weirded out. We hadn't been back more than ten minutes when the buzzer interrupted, a loud voice on the other end. A short, agitated black woman entered the room, was introduced as Faith, and said abruptly, "The pigs just bombed Panther headquarters in L.A. ! Unless you white folks get down to headquarters here right now, word is out that the same shit is gonna happen!"

I had some idea where this was coming from: I'd read Malcolm, Cleaver, Fanon, and talked frequently with my

friend Gil, a Panther out of Chicago. I'd even listened to three
of Malcolm's speeches Gil had on tape and read the Panther
newspaper and the Weathermen newspaper out of Chicago.
The first night on the road I had called Anna – Gil had given
her the details of the Chicago shootings of Fred Hampton
and Mark Clark – that it was basically an assassination. The
FBI and cops had been shooting up Panther offices on a regular basis ever since Newton and Seale had started things in
Oakland back in '67. So I figured this woman wasn't just crying wolf. Gil had told me, not long ago, "You are my good
friend, man, but some day I might have to kill you."

Janice said, "What do you mean?"

Faith said, "Unless you come down there and stand in front
of the building, the pigs are going to hit us. But they're not
going to take out a bunch of whities!"

I could see the look of fear in Laxton's eyes, even though
he was wearing his shoulder holster. Might not sit too well
with the cops if they searched him. I wouldn't have minded
witnessing *that* scenario. Janice said, "Let's go, guys!"

Obviously Laxton couldn't stand to lose face now. We
grabbed a couple of umbrellas and followed Faith down to a
deserted bend of Fillmore. There were already about twenty
people cordoning the Panther headquarters, mostly white.
They stood around, smoking, palming joints. After about an
hour I counted 36 people – 30 of them white. People from
inside brought us coffee. It was pretty spooky – not a sound
except our murmuring. Not a single car passed. Another half
an hour and a tall authoritative guy came out and said, "We
think the heat is off. If some of you want to stay, that's cool,
we'd really appreciate it. We could use a hand inside with
some mailings."

Janice, Laxton and I sat at a long table stapling flyers and
stamping them until she said, "I'm for calling it a night." We

said good-bye to Faith and the authoritative guy thanked us. We trudged back through the misting rain, not saying much. Laxton had lost some of his momentum.

I had developed a serious headache. When we got back Janice lit up another joint. I said, "Not for me. I'll have to excuse myself – way past my bedtime." I went into the bedroom, peeled off my clothes and got into bed – Janice's bed. And waited. Laxton and Janice kept talking animatedly, smoking and joking. Then I heard the conversation drop off, then stifled moans and the rhythmic movements on the leather couch of Laxton and Janice getting it on. My instinct was to get out of there right then, but where would I go? I pretended to sleep. My heart was broken. Broken? Heart? Janice came in about an hour later and was snoring in no time at all.

I lay there until about 7 AM, got up, hurriedly threw my stuff together and went out to a pay phone to call my buddy Frank down in Palo Alto. I explained the situation to Frank, who said he'd come get me in about an hour. When I returned to Janice's block I took up a spot on the corner to wait for Frank. Janice came down soon after, very contrite. Hugged me and said she was very sorry. I more-or-less stone-walled her, but said I was going to stay on the street and wait for a friend to pick me up. A friend. Janice left in tears. Then Laxton came down and said, "I'm really sorry about this... I wish I could take it back... I imagine you'd rather not make the drive back with me." I hadn't even thought about that. "Here's enough money for plane fare to Madison – it's the least I can do," he said. I took the money in silence, not even making eye contact with him.

The next day I was on my way back to Madison. I'd gotten bumped up to first class and was sipping a double Scotch. I had nothing to read, nothing to do. The seat next to me was empty. Not sure whether I was looking forward to seeing

Anna or not. Not sure, about much of anything. Two lines kept replaying themselves in my head: "The rabbit's running in the ditch/ Oh, no – must be the Season of the Witch," and "Because something is happening here/ But you don't know what it is/ Do you Mr. Jones?"

It was at that moment I saw Mick Jagger's baboonish rictus on the back page of the tabloid across the aisle.

*

The following August 24th, just after 4 AM, Karleton Armstrong, Dwight Armstrong, Leo Burt and David Fine, anti-war activists, set off a bomb they'd made out of ammonium nitrate and fuel oil in a van near Stanley Hall, which was connected to the Army Math Research Center on the University of Wisconsin campus in Madison. The blast killed a physics grad student named Robert Fassnecht, a guy I knew slightly. There was a rumor that the person who'd put Armstrong on to the idea was Laxton. Why, we'll never know – he had conveniently left town by then, for San Francisco.

His Orient Liquor in a Crystal Glass

Comus, JOHN MILTON

When I came out here to Taos it was the first time I'd ever been to a place where there's no water. What I do is crazy: every other day I jump into my car and drive to the river, or some trickle in a dried-up *arroyo*, and it's really a joke, isn't it?

I've had some good times out at the Hot Springs in The Gorge, though. I was there a few weeks ago except I ran into some people who looked like...*rem*nants of the Manson family and they were rather frightening. We shared the baths with them. We left sooner than we had hoped to leave. I really didn't enjoy the baths with them, because I saw us as a *perfect* set-up. You know, four transient hip-types passing through, and there was this couple, and she was *just like* what's-her-face...*Sadie*, you know, Patricia Krenwinkel – the girls who had carved their foreheads, the ones who were on trial – Linda Atkins and those people; sub-normal intelligence, high strident voices, almost passive in their general patterns, but ca*razy* eyes!

And she had a little black dog, and she kept saying, "SAB-BATH! SABBATH!" ...You know, obviously "Black Sabbath" was her dog's name. And her old man had a carved *thing* over here on his arm, and they were going to build a fire, and he took out this *huge* machete and that's when I decided, well, we'd better go.

And I had my first paranoid flash *ever* – that I could actually be a victim. I went through a *lot* of flashes about it, thinking they are extensions of my politics – true anarchistic murderers, and even though I may be *simpatico* and my thinking may be similar to theirs...they are the drones of an anarchistic radical thing; you know, the ones who'd think nothing of the *doing*. Most of the people into theory would not do it. But *they* would do me just as easily as they would do the most beautiful girl in Hollywood who had millions of dollars. And I saw *that* and I thought, do I set myself up for sacrifice, do I feel guilty because I wouldn't do it even though I can *ordain*…murder with a political motive?

And I went through all those trips as I was in the baths with them and I had the stu*pid*ity to make small talk at one point – the "where ya from?" small talk? And do you know what he said to me?: "Reality." The typical *dumb* hippie answer. But it was so heavy to me at the time because I was seeing, I was feeling all those things from them, especially with that motif in the background. She didn't shut up, for a minute: "SABBATH! SABBATH!" That high strident idiot voice. Calling this little black grungy dog.

And I was just vibrating all over those hot springs. And he said, "Reality," and I jumped up out of the hot springs and threw myself into the river which was ice cold. And he said, "It feels like you're rubbing yourself all over with razor blades, don't it?" – as if I needed *more* cues. And so I started getting dressed. My friends and I were all *very* ripped, and I thought, well, I'm not going through a paranoid *trip*, am I; it's not just *me*? My friends are not as politically *aware* – we were all on the same level, but their involvement with radicals in the flesh was somewhat less than mine.

I started getting dressed, and finally walked over to my friends and said, "I'd really like to go," and the couple got out too and started getting dressed, and he brandished his machete and started doing some wood.

And she says, "Come on, Sabbath, you're next; he'll whack you next!"

And I was just going, "Ohhhhhhh…let's go, girls…*time* to *move*."

48

Did you hear about the social worker up in Montana a few years ago who was dismembered and eaten by two hippies tripping on acid? I can get off on that intellectually, but God! It was just an incredible flash to meet up with it. And to see if it weren't for a question of numbers but of just the fact that they started getting their clothes on and started being very casual about it, and I'm thinking, "Ah, quick escape."

And she says, "Ja walk down here?"

And I said, "No, we left our car just on the other side of the bridge." You know, so that we would be identifiable if they were planning anything – we had a *car*. I was really *into* it, to covering for us; I was scared shitless. I was scared because I knew there was a "Reality" like that. But did you understand what I said about them being an extension of my politics? An unthinking intellectual extension of it but then *some*body's got to do it. They would not necessarily have the capacity to discern that *we* might be *simpatico*. I was suddenly becoming a *Liberal* to their *to*tal radicalism. And I *ha*ted myself for that, because Liberals offer themselves; "I love you, I'm into what you're doin', man." I wasn't about to express that to them, but I felt myself becoming a Liberal in contrast to what they were into.

Well, all this went through my head within a matter of a very few minutes. Especially since I was stoned, I was supersensitive to anything shaking my stone…and this whole thing was really coming hot and heavy. And my other friends were not even aware of it. And they almost had to *talk* me *down* as we were coming out of The Gorge and I was telling them what was going down, and they said "Why did you leave so early?" – we were going to spend the whole afternoon there, and we wound up spending all of twenty minutes.

And I said, "Listen, you know, people like that *do* things. You may or may not know it, but that's a reality." He said "Reality" and I just about died. An incredible afternoon.

And then something good happened. We left Arroyo Hondo and went in the direction of San Cristobal and met this *very lovely* hippie chick. Very sweet – she was going up to the Lawrence Ranch to meet her old man who was at some symposium. They were both from the University of New Mexico, up at the Lawrence Ranch for a weekend. And we gave her a ride in the back of our small little compact station wagon. And she said, "Oh, I feel just like Cleopatra on my barge," in a voice that was tiny and warm and bell-like.

These three friends of mine were on their way to Mardi Gras. They were stopping in Taos for a couple of days and that's why I took them to the Hot Springs and San Cristobal...we were doing...the *area* for a couple of days. And it turned out she was from New Orleans. And one of the fellows *going* was from New Orleans and they knew some people in common. And as they talked I flashed on some of my private memories: the road raised like a backbone cutting through the white sand and the salt marshes, the tall trees with lace hanging from them, the wisteria, the azaleas, the small towns along the way with those dusky geezers sitting out on their porches – everything so warm and mossy. Then Jackson Square, and walking along the oceanway, or whatever it's called. But what I *really* got into the most were those narrow cobblestone streets with the dark cool gardens and those big sparkling ferns. And from there into the French Quarter with its *ter*ribly tiny streets and girly shows. I always got off on the street bands, too – the black street bands in their white cotton shirts, black pants, and they sweated a lot...and the hippie street bands. The whole place was more like a bunch of small towns run together – not really a city at all.

The last time I was there I'd been speeding a lot and came down with malaria and I have to write that off as pretty much of a bummer. But my *maiden* voyage there was just priceless.

I went down with Nathan and Big Nancy. Everyone in the streets was doing either heroin, acid or booze – we were stoned on coke, mostly. There was broken glass ankle-deep everywhere in the streets. Nobody was straight. As usual they'd shut off all the water in town (except in the ritzy hotels) and closed all the bathrooms. We soon got into drinking at the wine booths and pissing and shitting in the alley behind a gay tea shoppe. Nathan put us on to the caring centers – the crash areas the spiritual groups set aside – the Unitarians, the Hari Krishna people, the Quakers. We crashed at the Children of God place the first night.

I was in high drag with green eye shadow, a green sleazy dress and green glitter in my beard. Nathan was trying to be very butch and so was Nancy. We got right into the parades, too – playing in the dirt and garbage with the masses while the patrons held court from their balconies – throwing us beads and golden coins. And they would always flirt with us before they threw them. The highest number of bead necklaces anyone I know has ever gotten is eighty-four – that's quite a few.

Well, we were in the French Quarter *swirl*ing around under this one balcony *fighting* over beads and this one magnificent snaky black comes out dressed in green crushed velvet – with baubles hanging everywhere – tantalizing us with beads and other treats. And he pointed – at me – he'd singled me out. He pointed again and motioned toward the stairs. When I got inside, the place was unbe*lieva*ble; exotic people draped around and locked together in every combination imaginable. He took my elbow and escorted me through. I remember in the first room there was this huge black dude doing a red-head who was up on a table making a lot of noise. And there were three fish bowls on a coffee table, each filled with pills – every kind of pill you could imagine. I stayed for four days. It was all so…flamboyant.

Anyway, this was all just in my head; I didn't want to interrupt. She wasn't with us that long, really. We did manage to get stuck in that damned adobe mud part of the way up there, though. We took her as far as the Ranch and she walked the rest of the way. And right before she got out, after I had been *freaked out*...by evil, down below in The Gorge – it was just super-symbolic to me, you know, down in the depths of The Gorge, in the Hot Springs, then going up to the mountains – she said, "Oh, here." And remember *I* wasn't going to Mardi Gras; she didn't know that, though – as far as she knew all four of us were. She said, "Here, this is from last year's Mardi Gras," and she gave it to me. It's a bright shiny gold coin that's from the Parade, the Comus Parade. It has this Athenian temple on one side, and on the other side this big jolly god. With a big smile on his face. Which this little blonde angel had given to me. You know, as a contrast to the evil that was down below, this little girl on the mountain had given me this lovely joyous coin. And my day was complete.

I said, "I'm ready to go home and take a bath."

Fritz's Bear

When I was seven I was invited to spend the summer with my two uncles in Montana and took my first train trip, accompanied by my grandmother on my father's side. My grandmother insisted that I call her Granny. She was very Irish, and had red hair just like me. On the train I remember eating parsley in the dining car. And I remember a black conductor who would come through periodically and say, dramatically, "3,942 miles to GINZA!" I had no idea what this meant, and I suspect that not many others did either, but we all laughed anyway. He'd come through every hour or so, announcing the adjusted mileage to Ginza. My Granny opined that maybe he'd been "hitting the sauce." Then I slept most of the night.

We got into Logan in the morning and there was almost nothing there except a little brown Ford car, a four-door sedan, and this kind of a rangy-looking guy in bib overalls and cowboy hat, standing there – he was the only thing there – he had to be my uncle. I'd met him in Los Angeles, of course, but he looked *totally* different. So we get off the train and he comes to meet us with *down*cast eyes. I'm thinking to myself, this whole thing doesn't look all that friendly to me. The landscape is dry and dusty and terrible looking. Well, anyway, we get into the car and drive across the two or three sets of railroad tracks, and as long as we're there we might as well go ahead and see the main street of Logan, which is about two blocks long. We make a left hand turn on to Main Street, which consists of a *store,* and two bars. As we're driving down the street, we come up to this bar, which I can still go to today – it had batwing doors – and as we're approaching it, out the batwing doors comes this cowboy cartwheeling backwards, completely off the boardwalk, into the middle of the street and falls down flat on his back. And here comes this other guy blasting out the doors right after him and starts pounding on him in the middle of the street. The guy jumps up and they begin wrestling around and jabbing at each other. And here I am, seven years old, first time in Montana, and two cowboys are fighting in the middle of the street. This was perfect.

It was my introduction to Montana – an old brown Ford, my Uncle Fritz, and the fight in the middle of Main Street, Logan. So we drove on out to the farm and I spent the rest of the summer. Things got progressively better from the moment we arrived at the farm. My uncles Fritz and Hap were as accommodating a couple of guys as you would ever want to meet. It was simple – I was a boy, and they wanted me around – I think because they liked me, but probably more so because I was my father's son. And they dearly loved him – he was their oldest brother's son. Actually, then, they were my great-uncles.

My dad, Leroy, was raised in Three Forks. When his father was in college in Butte, they'd often send my dad back to stay with Hap and Fritz. So Dad had a deep attachment to them. And I became a kind of surrogate son to them. To their way of thinking, I was probably a pretty good son, in that they didn't have to worry about me.

This was our morning routine: my Uncle Hap always got up first – he'd walk up to my door and say, "Boy!" (I'd mumble something). "Time to get up!" Then he'd walk over to my Uncle Fritz's door and say, "Frank!" (mumble, mumble) "Time to get up!" Hap would have already started breakfast, which was always bacon (hand sliced from a slab), eggs floating in bacon grease – each egg had a crispy collar, which was my favorite part – and baking powder biscuits. There was always a coffee can of bacon grease pushed to the back of the wood stove, at the ready for cooking purposes, or if Hap wanted to add to it. He kept a 6 inch by 6 inch flat chunk of sandstone about 2 inches thick, used to give a fast sharpening lick or two to a dull knife.

We'd eat while they discussed, in a cryptic manner, what they were going to do that day. The rest of us drank out of clunky mugs, but Fritz preferred his coffee in a teacup with a delicate handle. Near the end of breakfast, he would heap as much home-made jam or jelly on a biscuit as surface tension would allow – his notion of desert – then he'd say, "Well, whattaya gonna do today, boy?"

They always included me in everything where they thought that I could fit, but many days I would be entirely on my own. I had hundreds of acres, a BB gun, and a dog that was an Australian shepherd cross. My dog's name was Pup – he was Fritz and Hap's dog, but he followed me around during the summers I was there. Pup and his older brother Spig were incomparable when it came to handling cattle and hunting. Fritz liked to tell a story about a cattle buyer who offered $100 for the pair after seeing them work. This seemed an incredible sum, since they'd been given the dogs. They refused, of course. I doubt that actually paying money for a dog would have ever occurred to them, any more than taking an animal to a vet would.

Pup and Spig would hunt rabbits together – after jumping one they would take turns running it in circles until it was exhausted, then kill it. They'd tear it into two big chunks, lie down and eat. Spig was from an earlier litter. He was pretty creaky that first summer I was there, and he died just after I arrived the second summer. I stood there with Pup watching Fritz bury Spig. Pup disappeared for a week – we never figured out where to.

Once in awhile Fritz or Hap would be working maybe a mile or two away and I'd run over and jump on the tractor with whichever one it was and ride around for awhile then do something else. Fritz and Hap each had their own tractor. Fritz had a 1941 Poppin' John, won by a relative in a raffle up in Anaconda. The guy who'd won it, the husband of their sister Ann, had no use for it since he worked in the smelter there, so he just gave it to Fritz, who used it mostly for mowing hay. Hap, who was enamored of big machines, had an International WD-9 – the biggest farm-type tractor that International made at the time. Small as he was, he looked like a little kid up on that tractor; he could barely reach the pedals. He and the WD-9 got all the heavy work, but that's the way he wanted it. Way back, he owned a monster Buffalo-Pitts steam tractor. He told me that "You had to drag enough plows to get the ground up the first time." Meaning that the tractor was so heavy that if it went over the ground twice it would pack it down so hard it couldn't be plowed. Hap never exaggerated. And, of course, starting the tractors in the morning was a ritual that never varied. They didn't really have chores for me, but once I finally got to where I could drive the Poppin' John, two summers later, I'd rake the hay for them.

I was pretty much left to entertain myself, and I didn't have any problems with that at all. I came to understand that being by myself could really be a very nice thing, and that's stuck with me.

I lived a kind of free and easy existence with Hap and Fritz – I could go out and hunt jackrabbits, gophers, and birds – they didn't have a problem with my killing things – "oh, you're a kid – you can *do* that." A couple of years later I got a

. 22, a couple of years after that an Ithaca 20-gauge pump –
we'd moved to Redding by then – Fritz came on a visit and
helped me pick it out.

Or I could fish. Or I could just look at rocks. Or I could
go fall in the creek. They trusted me to take care of myself,
except I had to be there for lunch in the afternoon, and dinner
in the evening. I went up there for six summers in a row, from
1949 to 1954. So I had two family situations that were totally
different: for nine months a year I lived in California with my
mom, dad and brother and went to school, and for three
months I was with my uncles, roaming around doing as I
pleased. I thought it was wonderful. How could you ask for
more?

My great-grandmother lived with Fritz and Hap – she died
the second year I was there. And my granny lived in Three
Forks, in *town*. They would round me up once a week or so,
and say, "Okay, you're going to go to town to stay with your
granny."

"Oh, no," I'd groan. See, town wasn't where I wanted to
be. I remember nothing in particular about my visits to town.
I *do* recall that Granny was a stickler on bowel movements –
if you hadn't had one, out came the castoria. I figured that
one out pretty quickly. And once she sent me to the store,
and as I was passing by the yard where the Degidio kids were
playing, Junior Degidio shot me in the back with his BB gun.
I think he still lives in Three Forks. That first summer I remember playing with a girl who was a year older than I was,
and there was a kid who was a few years younger named
Frankie Parker who hung around us but never talked. I
thought that he might be mute. I got to know a few kids around
there, but my personal experience of the Huck Finn life was
the loner version.

Fritz and Hap were a pair – they were both really good

people. Fritz was more personable – you'd walk into a room and you'd know Fritz was there. He was a conversationalist. Hap was much more reserved, yet deeper. Hap was a reader – he'd gone to college for a year, Missoula, but the money didn't work out – the Depression and all. I remember one time when *I* was in college and I went back to visit them with a friend of mine –and we were talking about communism – at that time it was a big deal – we were talking about the Communists being a threat – and I remember Hap saying, "Well, you know, you can say what you want to about communism, but, you know, its been working pretty well for quite a little while now." He wasn't the sort of person you'd go over and start talking to, unless you knew him, probably, because he didn't volunteer a lot. But he thought things through. And he was pretty damn liberal. He had a framed photograph of FDR – abso*lute*ly. FDR was a whole lot more important than Christ. Absolutely.

Fritz and Hap were raised pretty much around the Three Forks area. They grew up in hard times. Their dad, Waddy Thompson Mongold, brought the family out from South Carolina – Fritz hadn't been born, and Hap was very young. They grew up in a little cabin that my great-grandfather built out on Willow Creek. Fritz's given name was James Franklin Mongold. Hap called him Frank and I don't really know where the Fritz came in. Hap's real name was Gladys Thompson Mongold. I have *no* idea where the Gladys came from, although the South seems to have a penchant for coming up with androgynous or at least peculiar first names. He got a *lot* of flak over that. He did. He insisted on being called Tom. Everybody knew him as Hap, but if you knew him well, you called him Tom. You didn't call him Gladys. He was diminutive, but he insisted on things, and he was tough. I'd say he was just under 5 foot 6, whereas Fritz claimed to be 6 feet. I once measured Fritz against the doorjamb and he stretched himself out to be 5 foot 11 and three quarters.

As I mentioned, Fritz and Hap lived with my great-grandmother. She was heavy, and just a shade taller than Hap. She didn't say much, and I didn't pay much attention to her. She died that second summer, at the age of 86. I remember it as being a Sunday. My grandmother was there to help her prepare a large dinner for us and other family members. She was in the kitchen most of that day. To me, she seemed old, and to move slowly. There was a full-sized watermelon on the linoleum countertop next to her, and as she worked she'd cut off a round, which she'd slice into wedges and eat ruminatively. Every time I came through the kitchen she was eating watermelon. By evening she was moving even more slowly than usual. It was hot, the dog days of August. I remember sweat drops in the hairs on her upper lip, and that her eyes were darker than usual. I detected pain in her expression. I don't know whether she ate the whole watermelon herself, but by evening it had been completely consumed. Dinner was uneventful, then our relatives left. Great-grandma said she didn't feel good and went in her bedroom to lie down. Granny started cleaning up. And within an hour Great-grandma had stopped breathing. I remember going out into the back yard and seeing Fritz by himself, crying. I left him alone. It was clear to me that eating all that watermelon had killed her.

Neither Fritz not Hap ever married. Great-grandma had the reputation of being a domineering woman and people told me that she would have been critical of almost any woman they'd have brought by. That was at least a factor, but I didn't know them as sexually active young men. Now and then Fritz would talk about the old days when they'd hitch the old road to Butte and spend a day or two. There was always a hint that they'd spent some of that time with prostitutes.

But they went through a lot along the way – they grew up in that country, they were part of it. They both worked at the Trident Cement Plant for more than 20 years – and there was always the farm – that's where they lived – that's the ground that they grew up on. And everybody else either died off or moved away – they were there, their mother was there – maybe it just sort of grew into something. I never asked them directly – I don't think anyone ever did. That wasn't the sort of thing you asked a person; "Why didn't you ever marry?" It's going to remain a mystery – having a strong mother that disapproved – that can't be the entire answer, because they were both intelligent people that would have understood "I *can* get away from this" – but it was the confluence of them h*aving* the ground, and *working* the ground and living there all their lives and –I don't know, I just don't know – Everybody says, "Oh, what a shame." Well, hell, I don't know that it was a shame – maybe they were born to live out there as bachelors the rest of their lives – I don't think I ever heard them argue. By the way, Mongold is a German name, but as I've said there was some Irish, and also a strong dose of Norwegian from my mother's side. There is, of course, the comic stereotype of the Norwegian bachelor farmer, although Fritz and Hap weren't Norwegian. And, anyway, being a bachelor or an old maid wasn't that uncommon in those days.

They would go in to town together, but do different things. Rodeo Days, for instance, is a *big* deal in Three Forks – a weekend in the middle of July. This was an occasion to actually take a shower, get out the straight razor and strop it up and lather and shave – spruce yourself up – new hat – go to town. Fritz would immediately go to the bar and start bullshitting with people, that was his thing. Five minutes after you'd get there Hap would be somewhere in the back in a poker game. They'd just go their separate ways. And around

2 o'clock in the morning they'd meet back up at the truck and go home. I can remember this quite well, because they'd bring me too. Main Street was free range – I'd be walking around with this bunch of drunks, through bars, and out in the street, fights erupting here and there. Keep in mind I was still a kid. Fritz would be in one place and Hap would be two bars away. You couldn't keep track. But eventually they'd hook up.

My grandmother would go with us to the actual rodeo. I remember sitting with her and Fritz, mostly, while Hap was off playing poker. Hap and Fritz would sometimes supply calves for the roping events but most of the stock was from the Lanes and the Buttlemans. My wife Bette and I were back at the Three Forks rodeo, in '77 I think it was, and they announced the winner of the bucking horse contest: Frank Parker – a familiar name. I went over to check him out and sure enough it was Frankie Parker, the little kid who didn't talk. I'm 6 foot 3, and he was several inches taller. I introduced myself and he began talking a blue streak – I actually had to make up an excuse to get away after awhile.

I continued to see Fritz and Hap as *often* as I could, up through the time I was in college at Missoula. Everything I've told you so far should give you some kind of context for the bear. From that first summer in Montana when I was 7, once a year it seemed, Fritz would take me through his bedroom into the big storage closet in which they kept stuff they'd accumulated over the years. Clothes, and hats, and some guns. There were probably half a dozen guns in there, mostly hunting rifles, and my grandfather's Winchester Model 12, known as "The Cornshucker" – a 5-shot pump, which had an exposed hammer – I have it now. Anyway, Fritz would always bring out a little box that had two teddy bears in it. One he would pick up very carefully, and the other one he would just point to. I could tell that the little bear he'd bring out was very important to him. He would cradle it like a child would. I can see him standing there, a middle-aged man in a beat up straw hat, bib overalls, permanent Copenhagen stains down the corners of his mouth, and about a week's worth of beard, cuddling this little teddy bear. It was a toy that his mother had bought him when he was a little kid and he'd look at it, and talk about it a little bit then put it back with its companion until the next summer, when we'd repeat the ritual. After the second time he ignored the other bear completely.

I remember this little bear so well. And *every year* we would go in and look at the stuff in the closet because probably he had forgotten he had showed it to me before, and he wanted to make sure that I shared this part of our history that was kind of important.

It was a common closet for both Hap and Fritz, and it was neater than what you'd expect of bachelors, who tend to keep stuff around in piles. I don't remember much else that was in the closet. But I was shown that teddy bear probably every year. And he always handled it the same way. With ultimate care. The way it looks now is exactly the way I first saw it back in '49.

The stuff in the closet was the *important* stuff. There were a couple of big trunks out in the chicken coop they'd probably moved out there after Great-grandma died. I imagine they thought, "Oh, maybe we'd better not throw these things away." There were sepia-toned photos, letters, and even stock certificates. I went back out there many years later with the intention of possibly resuscitating the stock certificates, but they had been eaten by mice. I looked through these trunks often, on my own time. Only one item stands out clearly in my memory – when Hap was little he wanted to learn to knit, so Great-grandma taught him. There was a tiny black sock, 4 inches long, with a white band around the toe – Hap's handi-work. I spent more time looking at that than anything else.

I remember when Fritz died, I was working in Berkeley as a Food and Drug Inspector. The State of California under-stood that when a *parent* died you should be allowed to go home for the funeral, but that was the limit. Well, I talked with my supervisor and told him that my uncle in Montana had died. I said this: "He's every bit as important to me as my father – and I'm *gonna* go home – so whether it's legal or not, here, I've gotta do it." And he said okay. Yes, I was Fritz's surrogate son. Both he and Hap were certainly surrogate fa-thers to me.

Bette and I moved to Montana in '70, and we weren't mar-ried yet – this was sort of frowned on. But Hap was open-armed; he just welcomed Bette. He helped us in every way he could. He gave us a house, rent-free. He gave us a calf – he was wonderful. Bette came to love him. She once told me that she wished she could have been there when I was grow-ing up. Hap was a darn good dancer. He and Bette would dance up a storm in the bars around Three Forks and Belgrade, and when her parents came to visit, he got along with them real well, even though they had a completely urban sensibil-ity. He was always a lot of fun. He died in '87 – we had just moved to Bozeman. Hap was born in 1898 – he *thinks*. They didn't keep real good records; he wasn't embarrassed about not knowing when he was born. "1898… I think." Fritz was born in 1906. He died just about a month before Bette could have met him.

When Fritz died, nothing much was given away so far as I can remember. But when *Hap* died, then things got divided up. I don't know if he did this because he knew I knew about the teddy bear and I had talked to him about it, but my Dad wound up with the teddy. And then when Dad died and my mother was distributing things, Teddy was there. I'm sure I asked for him – he wouldn't have meant anything to my brother Rex.

He's not a particularly attractive bear – skinny, with a narrow snout, jointed legs and head, and there's a hump on his back – he fits the prototype of the second generation of Steiff bears, made some time between 1903 and 1907. "Worse for wear" would describe him best. The left arm has been replaced, the front paws operated on, and black denim slippers have been stitched over the hind paws. The bear has had significant abdominal as well as back surgery. Most of the mohair on his body has been worn off, except for patches here and there, as if he had been a long-suffering victim of mange. The head and belly are particularly bare. His leather button eyes are replacements – the left one is black, and bigger than the dark brown right one. I look at him now and I see Fritz holding him – and I see a mother, too, who built an arm, and little socks for feet – and she probably put the little button eyes on – she was careful because it was obviously important to Fritz. So, to me, it shows a mother's love, too. I never saw that side of her in the brief time I knew her.

Just last week I took the bear to a local expert. He pointed out to me that the bear doesn't have the metal Steiff button embedded in his left ear, nor is there any indication that he ever did. He acknowledged that the bear has all the features of early Steiffs. And the remnants of his fur are, indeed, mohair. He said there were patterns that you could buy at the time, and that this bear was probably homemade. But I can't imagine who would go to this much trouble to make a stuffed bear for a kid, especially on a hardscrabble ranch in Montana. So it seems unlikely that we'll ever be able to authenticate Teddy's origins definitively. We're not talking about the Shroud of Turin here, but it would be nice to know.

Rock and Fire

I was maybe eight or ten miles down the road after leaving Ft. Sill, driving along at a normal highway clip, when I just started taking off my clothes and throwing them out the window – my shirt, my pants, got out of my boots and threw those out, too – and there I was cruising along in just my shorts and socks. I can't remember at what point I got dressed in civvies, but it just felt really good to shuck that layer of Army issue.

It was late June of '68. I was a free man again. I'd returned from a hitch in Korea, commanding an artillery battery, and finished out my last three months at Sill. I was on my way to Baja California to do some rock hunting – something I'd fantasized about since high school.

I'd first gone rock hunting during one of the summers I spent with my great-uncles up in Montana. There was a hired woman working for them named Gail who had three teeth, wore overalls and drove an old beater of a pickup. Once a week we'd load up in her truck and go looking for Montana blue agates. We always found some and it was always a thrill, for both of us. From that time forward I've had a tendency to snoop around on the ground and at least look at rocks whether I knew what they were or not. I didn't really get serious about this until I was in college and began educating myself. I guess it must be in my blood, too – my grandfather graduated from the School of Mines in Butte and became head geologist on the Ft. Peck dam project.

In California, when we were kids, the gold mining mystique was still strong, and legends such as the "Lost Dutch-man Mine" piqued our fantasies. It was also the time when private pilots flew over the land with Geiger counters, trying to locate uranium. In westerns, prospectors were always de-picted as Gabby Hayes-type hermits who lived on lizards and alkali and came to town once a year, speaking in tongues. Since I liked doing things on my own, I guess I identified with the curmudgeonly aspect of all that.

During high school I'd met a fellow named Otis who was married to my second cousin. He had been down in Baja with friends – they'd taken three jeeps – and he just raved about how much fun they'd had, and what interesting country it was. While I was going to school in Missoula I started read-ing up on locations and discovered that there were pegmatites in the Baja; I decided that when I got the chance, I was going to have a vehicle that would get me down there.

Every rock you pick up is a little piece of history, and a specimen from a particular location is going to be distinctly different from one found in another place. I was particularly interested in gemstones, especially those that are sometime found in pegmatites. Pegmatites are coarsely crystalline gran-ite and normally of little or no value, as they usually consist primarily of quartz, feldspar and mica. Occasionally, under the right circumstances, trace elements may be introduced during their formation, and if the proportions of these are just right, rare and sometimes valuable minerals may form as well – tourmaline, beryl (aquamarine, emerald), topaz and zircon, to name a few. Several gemmy pegmatites have been found in San Diego County in Southern California. The mines there have produced a large quantity of beautiful, valuable tourmaline. The sites in San Diego County are almost identi-cal to rock that extends down into Baja and forms a mountain range where they had indeed found deposits near a place called

Pino Solo. This is what prompted my relative to go down there and for me to be interested.

Well, I had planned to go to Baja after graduation from college but it was impossible because I was drafted right away and went straight to basic training at Fort Ord, California. You have your choice of artillery, armor, infantry, or engineers, and artillery sounded like you were several miles to the rear, firing the big guns. I definitely didn't want to be an infantryman slogging through the mud with a rifle, and I didn't want to be in a tank, because I knew the average life span of a man in a tank in combat is about 13 minutes, so I volunteered artillery and got it.

Prior to going into the Army I went through all sorts of considerations, even going to Canada. My brother Rex got out because he couldn't hear high notes. I don't remember whether he tried to join, or came up for the draft, but he was 4-F. My own rationale was if you're going to live in this country then the appropriate thing to do is just obey the rules. Get drafted and hope you live. You're only going to be in combat for a year, and you can probably squeak by if you're careful.

Basic Training was a couple of months and then another month and a half of Basic Artillery Training, primarily on the 105 Howitzer – from there they sent me to Leadership Training. While I was in Leadership School I was still an enlisted man, a private, but I'd applied for Officer Candidate School and it came through. I'd applied for OCS because I recognized early on that I wasn't going to be able to take orders from those bull-necked sergeants – I'd have wound up in the brig. Couldn't do it.

After six months I graduated from OCS as a second lieutenant, and they singled me out to go to Target Acquisition School – another two months. We were trained in methods of acquiring enemy targets on various systems – sound ranging, flash ranging, radar. In addition, there was survey information — you had to have absolutely accurate information for locating your guns. And weather information was essential, too.

The range and accuracy of the guns we were trained on amazed me. There was the 175 mm *gun* — we called it a *gun* because it had a long-range flat trajectory of 30 miles — you could shoot at Three Forks from Bozeman — and drive home a ten-penny nail. But this was a long time ago, before so-called smart bombs. Everything's relative.

We were told that we might have to call in fire on our own position. In an artillery unit, you're supposed to be away from the immediate action. But occasionally it happens that all of a sudden you're being swarmed by opposing infantry. The reason you would call in fire on yourself is that you are dug in and they're not. And in fact, if you are in a self-propelled unit — they put these Howitzers on vehicles too — one unit can point itself at the other and shoot off what is called a Pleshette round — a bunch of little tiny daggers. You just wipe off the personnel — it doesn't hurt the vehicle. It's happened a lot and you're most likely going to kill some of your own guys, but you're going to kill more of the *other* guy.

Most of my ocs class went to Vietnam because that's where the action was — this was in '66 — so it was heating up and they needed a lot of people because they were losing a lot. But as it turned out in the target acquisition battalion I was assigned to, there were about half a dozen officers in Korea that needed replacing because they were rotating back to Fort Sill. Well, that's probably why they sent me to Target Acquisition School in the first place — I didn't think about it at the time. From Target Acquisition School it was on to Jump School at Fort Benning, and then we shipped out to Korea. I felt like I had lucked out. It was a relief to go to Korea. To me that was like a vacation, because I liked the people and the country – aside from the fact that I was in the Army, it was fine. I'm no patriot. I was a patriot because I had to be. I was a good soldier, a good officer. I took pride in my work and I did it well.

Most of my time in Korea was uneventful. I went into the DMZ a couple of times to do some survey work – I had to get things set up and get out quickly. The DMZ was a two-mile-wide strip with huge fences on both sides, and bunkers and checkpoints as you approached. Nobody was supposed to be in there. My first time, they had arranged for me to rendezvous with a South Korean army officer. I got to the gate in my jeep and waited for him. And then I saw a little dust cloud coming down the road, and this guy comes busting up over the top of the hill with one hand on the windshield and one on the machine gun – just like George Patton. He jumped out and was all business. I was supposed to follow him, and my driver was busting butt trying to keep up. We got to their little camp nearby – they were camped where they couldn't be seen. There was a little war going on at that time. And at night they'd have monster firefights in which you'd see bullets and artillery rounds pouring into the DMZ – if you were in there you'd be pulverized. I met some South Korean Marines who actually stayed out in the DMZ.

Most of what I learned in Target Acquisition School I didn't have to concern myself with except for the survey. The battalion that I was assigned to in Korea had a headquarters for the battalion and headquarters battery with that battalion in one location and then it had two line batteries. Those are the guys with the sound ranging, flash ranging and radar – the headquarters battery that I commanded didn't have any of that but we had meteorological gear and survey. Our mission was primarily support for the battalion. So I spent a year there and came home just before the Pueblo incident—they froze everybody in Korea when that happened.

I never did take any leave when I was in Korea so when I got stateside I stopped to see my folks in Redding. They'd promised to help me with a new car when I got out of college and, of course, I had no use for a car in the Army. With the Baja in mind, I purchased a 4-wheel drive 1968 International Scout. Dad had a Scout, one of the first ones, a '62, and he was pleased with it – it was durable, nothing fancy, with good strong equipment on it. So I drove my Scout back to Fort Sill. I had three months left on my two-year commitment after OCS as an officer – gravy time in which to prepare for my adventure. Being out among rocks, some of them millions of years old, seemed like the perfect antidote to the impermanence of the military experience.

I built some cabinets, my first woodworking project; they looked absolutely horrible, but they worked. I could store canned and dehydrated food, and all my camping gear. A buddy of mine in our motor pool "requisitioned" a 50-gallon gas tank out of a 2 and-a-half ton truck for me, and I had a shop in downtown Lawton bolt it down in the middle behind the seats. I didn't want to run out of gas and I didn't want to depend on 5-gallon gas cans. The fumes were pretty terrible and it was probably spontaneous combustion waiting to happen, but it never did. I had a 20-gallon water tank, too. I came to use very little of that water because it smelled like the enamel they'd coated the inside of the tank with.

I bought most of my gear outside of Fort Sill in Lawton. They had two of the best stores I've ever seen, called Surplus City, north and south, with liquidated stock from hotels and tool companies and honest-to-God real Army surplus. Everything there was top of the line and cheap. I bought frying pans, a white gas cook stove, a hydraulic jack, a complete toolbox, and lots of canned food, mostly chili, to which I still have a slight aversion.

I'd been an outdoorsman most of my life, so I wasn't going to Baja as a beach boy – I took the proper clothing, but nothing really special. I bought a good pair of boots, a little compass, a small first aid kit, flashlight, flares, small shovel, rock hammer, magnifying lens, good maps, and I already had a good pocketknife and a . 22 rifle. I also got a good sleeping bag and a cot. I would sleep in the open because it never rained in Baja.

There was a dealer in Lawton who had a shop with a lot of nice guns – no shortage of weapons in Lawton. I bought myself a new . 357 Colt Python and a holster to go with it. I wanted a good gun. I can't remember what I paid for it, but it was pricey. Of course I wasn't supposed to take it into Mexico and I wasn't supposed to bring it back in the United States either, but I kept it in the bottom of my toolbox and nobody asked me about it and I didn't say anything about it. At that time it wasn't a big a deal. A friend told me that, when he took commercial flights in those days, he always stashed a pistol in his carry-on bag. So I took the gun along. I never did use it.

Everything fell in place nicely. By the time I was out of the Army I was ready to go. I didn't have a job waiting for me – my time was an open window. I had written the Mexican government and gotten their equivalent of USGS maps, and I had my source books, which included the approximate location where the pegmatites had been discovered.

*

I was in high gear, chain-smoking Luckies all the way to the border. I crossed at Mexicali, then went due west to La

Rumorosa. I took a decent dirt road following the west slope of the mountains – it was clear that I would need to pay close attention because the road signs were basically non-existent. I wound up near a town called Ojos Negros, then got on the main road. Fortunately there was a small hand-painted sign for El Alamo, otherwise I would probably have missed the turn-off. The map indicated seven or eight mines out that way. At a fork in the road four miles in I was to look for a single pine tree – Pino Solo. And sure enough there it was, on a ridge, though it had recently fallen over. I searched around for a good campsite, back and concealed from the road. I was here – this had been too easy. I made a fire, fixed myself some dinner on the camp stove and slept deeply under the Baja constellations, awakened only once by a nearby coyote's psychotic litany.

The next morning I got up and began my search. There were pieces of pegmatite scattered on the ground, and I could see where others had dug away at a long dike of pegmatite. This first day I would just scout the area.

On the second morning I dug into a likely place along the dike and was down about three feet when I broke into the roof of a pocket, and crystals of quartz, tourmaline, feldspar and mica broke loose under my pick. I dug through the clay layer carefully and got to the bottom of the pocket where I found lots of pieces, none of them distinguished. But this whet my appetite. In the afternoon I took another guess and this time, voila! I scraped away the shards and crystals at the bottom of a pocket, and there was a double-terminated tourmaline crystal. It was flawless, about three inches long, as big around as my thumb, raspberry-red at one end and sea-green at the other. I widened my hole excitedly, but there was nothing else there except scraps.

Late that afternoon, I was standing by the Scout wearing

my pistol in a holster on my belt, when two locals came through, driving a ragged bunch of cows. One of the guys noticed my pistol and said, "Hmmm....nice...gun... nice...gun." And I thought, maybe I shouldn't have had it out there like that. I had a flash to the banditos in *The Treasure of Sierra Madre*. I'd been warned that there were some pretty unsavory characters off the main road.

I left the Pino Solo location the morning after two full days there, and drove down to San Felipe just because I wanted to have a look at the country and take in the Gulf of California. The road from Pino Solo to San Felipe, though it was marked as a national highway, had absolutely no traffic. I remember stopping to get some beer at a tiny garage with a gas pump in front. It was surrounded by half a dozen little shacks. The beer was probably Tecate – terrible stuff – like drinking razor blades. It's better now, I think. There was an old man, his carbon copy son and grandson, and a skinny dog. I exchanged pleasantries with them, using my high school and phrase book Spanish, and a good bit of gesturing and face-making, which they enjoyed.

I stayed in San Felipe for a couple of nights. It was a sizable town of 2,500 people at the time. I found a place right on the beach, took a shower, relaxed and ate. I didn't sample the nightlife. I hadn't done much of that in Korea and I still had no interest in it; I'll admit I was a bit of a square. I mostly stayed in my room, walked on the beach and went to the restaurant and maybe read a little bit, probably about rocks – planning out my next move. I remember when I got up in the morning and looked out the window at the beach – it had disappeared! There was a squadron of about 200 pelicans stationed on a sandbar about a quarter of a mile out; the tide had retreated that far. There were myriad shells along the beach – perfect specimens – a crab hiding in almost every one I picked up. And a small fleet of shrimp boats in the bay. I ate lots of shrimp while I was there.

I just wanted to be by myself. I doubt that I talked with anyone, even though there were Americans at the motel and out on the beach sunbathing and swimming. In fact there was one very tan woman in her 30s in a skimpy black bikini, seemingly by herself, who kept trying to catch my eye, but I avoided eye contact with her. No thanks – not this time.

I went for breakfast that morning – I ordered huevos rancheros – and I thought to myself, you like beer, so why shouldn't you have beer with your breakfast? I'd never done that – beer before noon – people were going to think, *jeez what an alcoholic*. But here I was where nobody knew me and it didn't make a damn bit of difference if I had a couple of beers with breakfast. And it was great! The eggs had lots of chilies, and they, combined with the beers, gave me a little buzz.

San Felipe was a sleepy place back then. I understand they get upwards of 100,000 people during Holy Week and almost as many for Spring Break these days. And they have those damn races, several of them now – the 250, the 500, the 1,000. They'd just started them a few years before I went down there. When I was outfitting the Scout at Sill, guys would ask me where I was going and when I'd tell them they'd invariably say, mockingly, "Oh, ju go down ze Baa Haa!" It was a big deal by then and they'd all heard about it. But I couldn't have cared less.

So I packed up to do some more prospecting at Pino Solo again. I headed north on the highway up to El Crucero la Trinidad, then west. I was on the main road, which is now Highway 3, toward Ensenada. Several miles up the road I realized that I'd been fooling myself. This is a little bit embarrassing to admit – in the Army I'd been around a lot of people on a regular basis. When I got down there by myself, I found out that I really felt lonesome. This was something that wouldn't have occurred to me before, because I'd always enjoyed being by myself and entertaining myself, but here I was in a foreign place, with no amenities and nobody to talk to – it was something that I hadn't foreseen. In addition to that, I'd have to park the Scout, in which I had everything I owned. And to walk away from the vehicle a mile or two worried me; plus the fact that I hadn't seen my folks and my brother. It had never occurred to me that I would get lonesome.

Well, by now I was convinced that it was time to go home. I'd had notions of myself as a Great White Hunter or explorer but it didn't turn out that way. I finally admitted that I just wasn't cut out to do it by myself. If I had been with somebody, or there had been another vehicle, I wouldn't have been afraid of breaking down. I decided I was done with prospecting – that one piece of tourmaline was reward enough. But I still wanted to see more of Baja. I bagged it and decided to drop down and cross back to the west, over the mountains to San Quentin, then south to La Paz.

I turned off before San Matias at a place called Choyall and headed south, on the eastern flank of the Sierra de San Pedro Martir. The first part of the drive took me through a dry lake called Laguna Diablo. I've never been up the road from San Felipe to Mexicali, but the photos I've seen of that landscape remind me of the land I was passing through – stark, lifeless, but achingly beautiful in a rusty sort of way. The mountains had some peaks that were in the 10,000-foot range and they, too, were possessed of the same starkness. A friend had told me that the playas around there fill with water, mullet hatch out, the waters evaporate, and you could find full-sized fish skeletons littering the dry beds.

Eventually life appeared – ocotillo, barrel cactus, compass cactus, pencil cholla, brittlebush, palo verde, palo brea, desert mallow, grandfather cactus, and some cardon cactuses upwards of forty feet. There was lots of mistletoe draped in the palo verde and palo brea. The sage was stubby and there were vast colonies of creosote bushes. Each colony seemed to emanate from a central mound, but there was a fair amount of space between bushes. I noticed that several of the individual bushes were black, as if they had been burned.

I've learned since then that creosote bushes multiply like mushroom fairy rings, with the parent eventually dying off. Creosote is quick to adapt, and grows where nothing else can, partially because the plants suck the nutrients out of an area, thereby inhibiting competition. The roots send out shoots – it just keeps getting bigger and bigger. There is a family of creosote bushes thought to be the oldest living beings on earth, at 11,700 years.

I got out and stomped around in the creosote – there were little burrows everywhere – lots of creatures made their homes among the roots. Everything had a fading, bedraggled look, as if it had just passed its prime the day before. It was hot, the second week of July – I didn't have a thermometer along, but it seemed to be in the low 90s, but comfortable. Where I lived, around Redding, it gets hotter than blazes, 120 degrees, the same as it could in Baja. I was young and impervious – I don't remember it being smoking hot, though. It could well have been up to 100 degrees. Not a single dwelling.

I came to a sandy track which shot off due south. The road wasn't marked at all, nor were any of the roads, but my intuition told me this was right. I was traveling a little closer to the mountains and there were more and more cardon now – huge buggers. I passed a rancho in the foothills, a rusted John Deere under a ramada – this was what I took to be marked as

Algodon on the map. Then another fallen-down rancho on the left, and some fields under cultivation. At the point on the map that indicated a turn to Agua Caliente there was a sizable rancho with burros drinking from a pipe and a small herd of skittish Brahma crosses – the bull gave me his best macho stare. This wasn't going to be my passage through the mountains, but I wanted to see the hot springs. About a half mile up the road, into the start of a small canyon, I came into a miniature oasis – a delicate grove of palo verde, and a tiny stream, surrounded by bonsai shrubs and flowers, trickling down through the rocks. Many of the plants and shrubs protected themselves with dramatic thorns, especially the datura – wonderful designs. The rancher had fashioned a small corral from old bedsprings turned on their sides.

I got out and followed the stream up to a rise where there was a cement tank filled to the brim. This was fed by a thin plastic pipe, which obviously ran from the springs. About a dozen bees were stationed at the edge of the water. I dipped some out and splashed it on my face and stuck my arms in up to my elbows – ecstasy! I was tempted to stick my head in and swallow long draughts, but thought better of it. There was an arroyo below which cut a huge sandy swath. If you happened to be down there during a flash flood you'd be in for a wild ride. I walked up the road another half mile, but it was apparent that the springs were still some distance ahead, so I decided to turn back. There were motorcycle tracks in the sand. A friend had told me that hot springs were often places where growers had their dope plots. While I was armed, I wouldn't want to confront the growers association with the odds in their favor. Back at the tank, I soaked my bandana, tied it around my head, and then backtracked to the "main road." I would continue south a bit until I'd passed the tail end of the mountains, then cut west and find my way to a good campsite.

What I had was the Mexican equivalent of a USGS map. It had all the roads, from the good ones down to the bad ones, then the worst roads which were just dotted lines. Initially I had been on a recognizable road, but I wound up following dots to the west. There was a kind of track, but it wasn't really a road —well, maybe in just a few places. Anyway, my plan was to follow the dotted line all the way across the mountains and down into San Quentin on the Pacific.

It was in the area south of Agua Caliente that I started to notice something peculiar. I saw smoke coming from a creosote bush, like a little campfire that was just about to go out. Then another, farther down the road. At the third one I got out to take a closer look – the bush was actually smoldering.

I decided to swing west, and immediately put the Scout into transmission combined low as i started to climb. Now I noticed more and more of the smoldering creosote bushes. When I got to the highest point, on a little mesa where I had a 360 degrees panorama, I stopped to camp for the night. I set up my cot, rolled out my sleeping bag, made a little fire from dead ocotillo, then cooked some dinner on my camp stove.

It was dusk, 9:00, maybe even 9:30, and I could make out little flickering fires, 50 to 60 of them, some in every direction. Now it wasn't just smoke. In most places, if you saw fires like that, it would be a matter of concern, but not here, where the vegetation was so sparse – mostly rocks, with little clumps of bushes scattered about. These fires were separated by an average of a quarter of a mile. I could see off a long ways and it was going on all over. Lightning wasn't the culprit – there'd been no rain for months, and no sign of any humans who might have lit the bushes.

As I finished my dinner, I spotted one fire, 30 yards from my camp, which had obviously just started up while I was cooking – this was getting weird. It wasn't a Moses and the burning bush kind of thing that just burst into flame, poof! , but it was still enough to make me uneasy. There was something aggressive about the fires, a threatening, living energy. Yet it was under control, waiting. There was no human element in these fires, unlike what you might see if you were looking down at the encampment of an ancient army. This was the antithesis of the night training exercises I'd been involved in, and the DMZ exchanges I'd witnessed in Korea, where explosions shook the earth and flashes seared your retinas. As unsettling as the fires were, at the same time I began to experience an abiding peace.

I was taking all this in, sitting on my cot smoking a Lucky, when I sensed I was being watched. Just then a roadrunner hopped into my camp, looking around, pecking at the ground here and there. I had heard that roadrunners were really timid, and I didn't want to spook the guy, so I just sat there holding my breath. I'm positive that he knew I was there, but since I didn't move he wasn't particularly cautious. Finally he hopped up to within 10 feet of me and looked out at the same prospect I'd been surveying. Maybe he was watching to see what creatures the fires would flush out. Anyway, we sat there like that, next to each other, for a good two minutes. I finally got tired of sitting still and thought I'd just get up and move around a little, but not too fast. So I stood up and he took a couple of little hops back and looked up at me to see what my next move was. I went around organizing stuff for the evening, scrubbed out my frying pan with sand, while he continued hopping about the camp until he got bored with it and left.

The night was completely silent. Not a single sound. I eventually fell into shallow sleep, waking periodically to look at the fires – they were exactly the same. I had odd, disjointed dreams, and was exhausted when I got up in the morning. When I descended the mesa several of the bushes still had hints of smoke floating in the air around them, but there were no more flames – the bushes were, however, blackened. I found no clues about the cause of the fires.

I was on my way. The ground flattened out pretty quickly and the going was easy. I remember eventually passing a place called Mesa Nueva York and coming down a drainage where the vegetation was quite lush. There was a small airport and I got spooked because I thought it might be a drug operation.

When I hit Highway 1 at San Quentin, it was like one bomb crater after another; the Scout was bottoming out, so I decided to treat myself to a rest. I had planned on going farther south down the coast, but the road was such a disaster that I changed my mind – you could walk faster than a car could go. If you went off road, as many people had, those side tracks were just as bad, some worse.

I found a nice little place called the Old Mill Motel, maybe a dozen little units. The owner and his wife were Mexican citizens who'd retired from San Diego – they spoke perfect English and his wife was an excellent cook. He had a boat, a little sixteen foot outboard, but his wife didn't enjoy fishing, so he asked me along. The only thing I had was my trout rod, so I brought that and my little tackle box and we went out into San Quentin Bay. He was fishing for halibut and had a special rig he'd made up. I thought, well, I'll just fish as if I'm fishing for trout.

I cast around a bit and caught one. Then another – not huge but respectable. Meanwhile he hadn't gotten a nibble. So he borrowed some of my tackle and finally got one. Now we had three, enough for dinner. The wind was kicking up, it was a small boat and we were out there close to the mouth of San Quentin Bay – we decided we'd better go back. So he started the motor, pushed the throttle forward and nothing happened. In the course of our conversations, I'd learned that this guy was a retired chemical engineer; nevertheless, he threw up his hands in despair and grabbed an oar and started paddling – it was at least three miles back to the dock and there weren't even oar-locks on the boat.

Now, I'm not the world's best mechanic, but I thought, let's see if we cant find out what's wrong with the motor anyway. So I took the hood off the thing and saw that the pin holding the cable that moved the carburetor linkage back and forth had broken off. He didn't have any tools, not even a pair of pliers; no screwdriver, no clamps, no spare parts. I went through his tackle box and got the biggest fish hook I could find and cut the head off that sucker, then stuck it in the hole and bent it. It wasn't pretty but it was going to work. Well, he was amazed. What I should have done, of course, was get it started and then work the throttle by hand and let him steer. As it turned out, after I got it all connected, he started the engine then pushed the throttle all the way forward and we were bouncing across that bay plowing into chop after chop. The guy was so happy he wasn't stuck out there, and he wanted to get home as fast as he possibly could before anything else happened. All the way back I was afraid that he was going to capsize the boat. Anyway, we made it and had the halibut for dinner.

The next day, he wanted to go fishing in his boat with the fishhook throttle connection. But at that point I was running low on money, after having left the Army with my last paycheck and a little bit extra, and I thought, maybe I'd better go home and explore the possibilities of what I was going to do with the rest of my life. So I headed north. Poked around Ensenada – went out and had some fish tacos at La Bufadora after getting sprayed mightily by the blowhole, had a beer in Hussong's Cantina, where Monroe and McQueen (separately) used to hang out, and looked in the window of the Bar

Andaluz, which was closed, so I had to settle for fantasy images of the bygone clientele – Lana Turner, Myrna Loy, Delores Del Rio, Johnny Weismuller, Ali Khan, Dempsey.

I spent a week with my brother Rex in San Francisco and smoked marijuana for the first time. He asked me if I wanted to try it – I hemmed and hawed but finally took a toke or two and nothing happened. I toked a little more and all of a sudden a whole lot happened! Then I got a little nervous and paranoid. Rex said, "When I get that way I just go out and take a walk." So we went out and walked and he said to me as we were walking along, "You're walking like a lieutenant!"

Three or four years afterwards I was reading Carlos Castenada's *The Teachings of Don Juan*, and the sequels. Carlos and Don Juan would often venture out into the desert at night and see quite strange phenomena, including spooks of various sizes and shapes.

I put two and two together and thought, well, supposing the desert west of San Felipe is a training ground for apprentice *brujos*. Apprentices had tasks – a *brujo* might say to an apprentice, "go out there and start some fires." And these *brujos* were capable of shape-changing – maybe the road runner was actually a sorcerer who had changed shape and was checking me out to see if I was a potential danger or just a normal slug who happened to be camping in their bailiwick. Don Juan was fond of transforming himself into a coyote. In native stories, Coyote is sometimes brilliant, often a fool, now and then both. I'd never heard of anyone taking the form of a roadrunner, or of Roadrunner as a mythical figure, although his powers in the cartoon must have some basis. How is it that Wily Coyote and Road Runner got paired up?

Carlos was under the influence of several mind-altering drugs in those books, and when I've told my burning bushes story people have often asked me what I was on. At that point

I was a total straight arrow, unless you count Luckies and an occasional beer. Maybe it was Kokopilau messing with my head. I understand that most people regard the *Don Juan* books as bogus, but they had their place at the time. Yes, I was naïve in those days, and, yes, I knew it was a fanciful explanation. That was the only roadrunner I saw on my entire trip. And one pair of coyotes loping off the highway north of San Felipe.

*

It's been 35 years since my trip to Baja. I've lost my good map but recently purchased another and started trying to retrace my wanderings – few of the place names ring bells – too much time has passed. I can't find my dotted line, either – I suspect at least part of it was wiped out by Hurricane Nora in 1997.

The fires in the desert have puzzled me all these years and I'd like to find an answer. Consequently, I've begun asking people knowledgeable in matters related to Baja – biologists, ethnobotanists, tour guides, writers, or some combination thereof. A prominent botanist at a university in Mexico has not returned my email, but all the others have been interested and forthcoming, yet not one has had an explanation of substance. *A* has referred me to *B* who has referred me to *C*, and so on. So the doors continue to open. I'm in touch with a tour guide out of San Felipe who is going to ask some of the old guys out that way – this seems like the most reliable source, aside from going down there and asking them myself.

Two friends, one a professional chemist, told me the same thing when I spoke of the burning bushes – that the oil in creosote leaves is highly volatile and I may have been privy to an odd occurrence of spontaneous combustion. If this were true, one would assume that there is some positive outcome for the creosote as the result of this phenomenon. So far no one has been able to validate that these fires actually occur in the Baja, or why they would occur.

Another friend, a naturalist who has spent good amounts of time in the Baja, said that there are geothermal pockets under that area, and that might have something to do with the fires. He also told me that packrats nest in the bushes and pile up debris, but that it would take a lot of compression to start a fire in a packrat nest.

Recently, an entomologist told me of the existence of a relative of the silverfish and the firebrat, which lives, as far as he knows, only in the Baja and in one area along the Arizona-Mexico border. The firebrat, *Thermobia domestica*, thrives in high temperatures, but also needs moderate humidity. Somehow this new species evolved in areas where there is almost no humidity. This mutant, *Thermobia presbyterianus*, was first observed by Lyman Beecher, a distant scion of the famous Massachusetts family, but not the Lyman Beecher who was father to Harriet Beecher Stowe. This Lyman Beecher was a frontier missionary and evangelist for the Presbyterian Church and traveled in the southwest in the 1850s and '60s. He spent much of his time among tribal peoples along the Arizona border.

The motto of the Presbyterian church is *nec tamen consumabatur*, "Burning but not consumed" – relating to the burning bush witnessed by Moses but also to the early church's struggles during the English Reformation. One often finds this Latin phrase and symbol over doorways of Presbyterian churches in Scotland.

Beecher was out walking in the desert west of the Serrita Mountains one spring evening and noticed several creosote bushes burning separately but with some intensity. He interpreted these fires as a "Message from God." Beecher was a mystic, it is said, but also something of a natural scientist. And what he observed upon closer inspection was that the fires were not spontaneous but caused by *Thermobia presbyterianus*. He studied their behavior over the next three years and noted that neither sex is winged, but that during mating the male develops a clear convex appendage on his abdomen. Finding a suitable creosote branch during daylight hours, the male positions this appendage in line with the sun's rays and burns a series of holes in the creosote branch in which the female will lay her eggs. Natural selection favors those males that have the ability to burn the deepest and largest holes. However, on rare occasions, the inflammable resins in the creosote reach their flame point. My entomologist friend heard the Beecher story from his mentor, an expert on desert fauna, who died several years ago.

This sounded pretty bizarre, but I had a feeling of elation, knowing that my search might be over. I went on the Internet and found no record of Lyman Beecher, the evangelist and traveler of the southwest. Nor did I find any mention of *Thermobia presbyterianus*. This made me suspicious.

I called my entomologist friend and asked him about the veracity of his information. He admitted that he'd made it all up. It was a real letdown, and in a way I was angry that he had taken me for a ride, but the hoax was a good one – I had to admire it. And I still don't have any more of an explanation than I did 35 years ago.

Halters

One day in 1990, when I was visiting my friends Dan and Bette in Bozeman, Dan told me to come out to the garage; he had something he wanted to show me. He took down an ordinary-looking grocery bag from a shelf and handed it to me. Heavy. I opened the bag and took out two halters. At the time I didn't know a halter from a halter-top. The leather was in good shape, still pliable, and each had two big brass buttons, one on each side, with "U.S." raised on its surface.

Dan told me that his friend Jack Embree had given the halters to him and that now Dan wanted to give them to me. Embree had told him that the halters had been taken off dead mules on the Little Big Horn Battlefield, from Reno's ammunition train that day in late June 1876. Two boys had unearthed the halters in some kind of trunk in the 1960s.

Embree, who was white, was married to a Northern Cheyenne woman named Agnes, and through her an old Cheyenne man had given the halters to Embree, who no longer had any use for them and thought that Dan might, given that he had expressed interest in them before. Knowing that I had studied Indian history and culture and had contacts on several reservations, Dan had decided that I would have a better idea of what to do with them than he. Embree had died and Agnes had returned to the reservation.

I held the halters in my hands while Dan told me this. I remember that I could feel the skin on my back trying to crawl off. These were, after all, just old halters, but I had walked Reno's hill several times and had a pretty good sense of what went down that day, particularly from reading and listening to the Indian side of the story.

I had seen that day so many times in so many different ways: from the perspective of the huge encampment on the other side of the Little Big Horn; looking up as the warning came; charging down the hill with Reno, then retreating and burrowing into the earth; Reno getting splattered with the blood and brains of Custer's favorite scout Bloody Knife; riding in behind Custer then the plummeting feeling of certain death; taking it out on the bodies of the soldiers; the celebrations and the lamentations that night; watching from a distance the next day as two women came upon Pahuska's (Long Hair's) body and hammered the awl through his eardrum because he had not listened; the camp packing up and leaving; what the burial party encountered.

At the time, I was going through a particularly troubled patch in my life and I'm sure I wasn't paying close attention to the details of what Dan had been telling me. And now *I* was the one who didn't know what to do with the halters. I returned to my self-absorbed life in Iowa City with the halters in tow. Here I was in a town home to a factory that produced reams of the most compelling and shapely fictions, in possession of two patently humble objects saturated with stories much more vital.

In early October I had a two-week residency at the Ucross Foundation outside Sheridan. I borrowed a car and made several visits to battle sites in the area. I walked around Fort Phil Kearney, went to the scene of the Wagon Box Fight, the Battle of the Hundred Slain (Fetterman's Folly), and the Battle of the Rosebud. Starting with Red Cloud's resistance to traffic along the Bozeman Trail, many of the engagements with the Sioux and their allies had undoubtedly seemed ominous to the u. s. government. Standing on the ridge that Fetterman and his men had ridden across into an overwhelming ambush gave me some satisfaction, I must admit. The Rosebud site, more sprawling and remote, presented the opportunity to speculate where certain skirmishes had occurred, which I had read about in several accounts, notably those of Wooden Leg, who'd been involved in both that battle and the Greasy Grass (Little Big Horn). I wandered around Sheridan a bit, and spent time in King Ropes, one of my favorite stores. They have a small museum there, and in it I saw a halter identical to my two.

That December I walked the last day of the Bigfoot Memorial Ride (*Sitanka Wokiksuye*) commemorating the 100th anniversary of the massacre at Wounded Knee. The temperature, with the wind chill, got down close to 90 below. I could take only one photograph at a time before the shutter of my camera froze open. The riders swooped past toward the cemetery like ghosts themselves, both they and their horses with heavy white beards of frost. If part of the intention in retracing Bigfoot's route was to experience some personal sacrifice themselves, the riders had certainly done so. As we came down the road from Porcupine to Wounded Knee, we witnessed a double sundog, visible evidence that the Creator was watching. Black Elk had said of Wounded Knee that the Lakota Nation's hoop had been "broken and scattered," and that the people would suffer untold misery for seven generations – this had certainly come to pass. The ceremony at the cemetery that day was called "Wiping the Tears of Seven Generations." – the Nation's hoop was once again intact. The sundogs had been a sign.

It came to me while standing there at the cemetery, with the purifying smoke of sage and sweetgrass wafting over me, that rather than keeping the halters as curiosities I could bring out to show people, it would be more appropriate to get them back into the hands of the tribe which may have claimed them from the battlefield. At any rate, they represented symbolically one of the most monumental events in Northern Cheyenne history. This made sense to me, plus it got me off the hook.

I had contacts in Lame Deer who told me I should speak with tribal historian Bill Tall Bull, a direct descendent of Tall Bull, who'd been a combatant at the battle of the Greasy Grass. In dealing with any bureaucracy, you can expect a bit of a runaround, and in dealing with tribal bureaucracies, part of the runaround is that they need to size you up. Given the previous 500 years, that's understandable. Anyway, I called Bill Tall Bull several times before connecting with him. I explained what I had, about Jack Embree and Agnes, and that I wanted to return the halters to the Northern Cheyenne. He was cordial, but when I told him about the circumstances under which they were initially discovered, I could hear, in his voice, reservations about accepting them. He explained that someone's burial might have been disturbed, possibly an Indian who had been killed at Little Big Horn. Finally, though, he told me to bring them by and he would try to track down Agnes or anyone else who might know something about them.

The following August I passed through Lame Deer and delivered the paper bag to Bill Tall Bull. I found him at the tribal complex. He took me around the John Wooden Legs Memorial Library, which was part of Dull Knife Community College. I'd known John Wooden Legs, Cheyenne educator and medicine man, descendent of Wooden Leg. John had been a good man and an articulate spokesman. Bill Tall Bull told me that he would place the halters in a display case in the library with a note explaining the story, asking if anyone knew anything more about them. I felt that I had made the appropriate choice.

Two years later I was adopted into the Miniconjou band of the Lakota Nation in a traditional *hunkapi* ceremony at the community of Iron Lightning, South Dakota. Occasionally I would stop in Lame Deer to gas up on my way through to visit Dan and Bette, drive around a bit and ask about my old friends, but it was only in passing. This wasn't the most direct route, but that country still held an important place in my soul. I continued being actively involved in Lakota ceremonies and culture, but my association with the Cheyenne was fading.

Many years went by, and I never once stopped to ask Bill Tall Bull if he had found out any more about the halters. I had always had the nagging feeling that I hadn't done enough, that I had not played my part with attention or integrity. Had I turned my back on my responsibility?

Dan and Bette had retired to the Upper Peninsula of Michigan, so my trips to Montana became less frequent. I went to visit them in Michigan for the express purpose of having Dan tell me the story again, now that I was finally ready to hear it. This is what he told me:

Jack Embree was an over-the-road teamster, coast-to-coast. He retired having driven three million miles without an accident. He was always meticulous about his grooming, what he wore, his truck, his tool shed, his toolbox; everything had to be just right. His Dodge pickup was so clean that you could eat off it, inside or out.

Everybody around Three Forks knew Jack, but nobody knew him well. For some reason he singled me out to be his friend.

When Bette and I moved into the house in Three Forks it was surrounded by overgrown silver-leaf poplar that needed to be cut back. I got out there with the chainsaw and pruned them all down to where they looked like little kids' drawings of trees. I had tons of branches in the yard – bucked it all up and split it into firewood. Well, anyway, I noticed Jack out there watching me sometimes. He didn't say anything to me, he never came over. At the time, Bette worked in town at the Cenex station and she overheard him talking about "that big red-headed guy out there, a'choppin' that popple up – by God, you oughta see that guy!" To me it was just getting rid of the damn wood. Anyway, he was, for some reason, impressed with that. So we got to talking a little bit once in awhile. Well, then we got to where we kind of liked one another. I started calling him Embricci (EmBREEchee), and he liked that, then I took it a little farther and said –"You're not a reprobate – no, that's not the word I'm looking for – ah, now I remember…you goddamned rabble rouser, Embricci, anyhow!" Boy, he would just burst into laughter, he just loved that so much. Then he'd say, "That's me…yup…a rebel rooster, sure enough." He misheard me every time but I never corrected him. Out of all the people in Three Forks I think I'm the only one he regarded as a kindred spirit. Bette got to see him more often than I did because she worked at the Cenex – he'd always stop there and ask her how Big Red was doing.

I said he was meticulous about his appearance. One odd thing about Jack was that he had this thing on his chin, but you never knew what it was because in the morning he'd get up, shave, and place a band-aid across it, horizontally, exactly the same every day. You never saw him without it. There was always speculation about it around the Cenex, but it wasn't the kind of thing you'd go up to a guy and ask him about.

Well, just one little story about Embricci. His neighbor across the street had a dog, that was supposed to be contained, but it wasn't. The guy was a businessman downtown – he just didn't pay attention and this dog would come over and shit in Embricci's yard. For Embricci, the neatnik, this was absolutely awful – like somebody throwing beer bottles in the yard, but in a way, worse.

So he complained to the guy about it, a couple of times, and then not so politely, and the guy never did anything. Well, one day I was driving by and there was Embricci with his shovel vigorously scooping up the dogshit, carrying it across the street, and tossing it into the back of this guy's yard. That was the end of the problem. People in Montana treasure their dogs, but you'd better not let yours wander — particularly among your neighbor's livestock. People shoot without hesitation. At least this was settled peaceably.

Jack and his wife Agnes lived in a doublewide that was always immaculate. I never knew whether Jack had been in the service, but their trailer would have passed inspection any time, day or night. Agnes was Northern Cheyenne, from Lame Deer. She was pretty much a reservation Indian. She was a sweet woman, a little older than Jack, and wrinkled beyond her years — "a face like the Badlands," they used to say — in her case probably the result of chain smoking. She always seemed quiet and subservient. In several of our conversations Jack intimated that Agnes longed to go back to the reservation, but that he wasn't having any part of that. How they wound up in Three Forks I don't know.

Jack never drew Agnes into our conversations and my read of the situation was that she preferred it that way. So I didn't pay much attention to her. She took good care of Jack in the old-fashioned way — he seemed to be the focus of her life.

One day I was over at their place and he said he had some "stuff" he wanted to show me. He said "Well, I got these bridles..." He went to a shelf and took down an ordinary-looking grocery bag and handed it to me. In it were two halters (not bridles as he called them). The brown leather had been blackened by the passage of time, but it was still supple.

This was in 1980, so my memory of what he told me is pretty foggy. As best I can recall it, Agnes knew an old man on the

Northern Cheyenne reservation who had the halters, which had been found by two young boys with some other items in a trunk or other kind of container that had been buried at the Little Big Horn battle site. And I don't remember whether the old man wanted to give them to Jack or Jack asked for them. The halters had supposedly been taken off dead mules that were part of Reno's ammunition train. I'm not sure who buried them or where they were buried exactly, or when, or why.

He could see that I was fascinated by these objects, but then I just sort of let the whole thing go. A month later, out of the clear blue, Jack showed up with the paper bag and gave it to me. He didn't really say why, but it seemed it was because he liked me, because I was curious about the halters, and he didn't know what the hell to do with them otherwise.

Jack died suddenly about a year later, of congestive heart failure. After he died Agnes called up Bette several times, usually tearful – she just didn't know what to do with herself without Jack. Eventually she went back to the reservation and we lost touch with her.

I kept the paper bag on a shelf in my garage. Every time I'd pass by it I'd think to myself maybe these are valuable, maybe I should find out, maybe I should talk to someone who knows something.

Now I had at least one solid, though incomplete, generation of the story. My next step was to call the Little Big Horn Battlefield Museum. After several detours, I finally spoke with John Dorner, who told me that most of what had been left at the scene of the battle had been piled up and burned, and that any surplus had been used as draft equipment. He said that the Indians had stripped down any saddles they may have taken, and thrown away things such as bits and stirrups. He said that the site had been used as a hay cutting camp from

1877 to 1898 and was called Fort Custer. It had been occupied mostly by teamsters and quartermaster personnel, and that the Crow had moved over from Mission Creek and Rosebud Creek up near Big Timber to live around the area. Reno's ammo train did use mules, but that their halters included blinders and that the rosettes (the brass buttons) had teeth that pierced through the blinders. Some years later, he said, the buckles were japanned – iron which had been painted black. I didn't remember blinders on my halters – maybe they were actually from horses, not mules; both horses and mules had been picketed around Reno's position. If they were for horses, they were big horses. Why hadn't I at least taken photographs of the halters? He told me that some of the surplus tack from this period was still in use by the Forest Service into the 1940s. The most important thing he told me was what I already suspected – that the halters from that period were identical for about a fifteen year period, and actually authenticating that my halters had been there in 1876 would be an impossibility unless they had some personalized markings. And, of course, I didn't have them to offer for examination. Mr. Dorner had given me clear information and had been generous with his time and patience.

I knew that Bill Tall Bull had been having health problems. I called the Tribal offices in Lame Deer and asked about him. The young woman who answered the phone told me that he had passed away four years ago. I asked if anyone had taken over his duties. She said that Bill's son Linwood was doing that now, and gave me a number at the tribal complex to call. He was there, and his voice was young and energetic. I told him my story, and that the halters had been in his father's keeping. He said that he himself had never seen these halters, but he had a lot of sorting to do; there were 29 boxes of his dad's files to go through and maybe something would turn up. I asked him whether he knew of an Agnes Embree, who had been married to Jack Embree. He asked the women nearby and they said yes, she was around. Another minute into our conversation he said, "Oh, they just told me that she's right here, playing bingo…After she's done, in maybe 15 minutes, I'll bring her in here and we'll call you back." I waited for half an hour. There are jokes about "Indian time," and I had had numerous experiences with it and had come to accept it as a reality. I had to leave to pick up my son from school, so I called Linwood back. He said that the woman they thought was Agnes Embree was someone else, but that he'd "put out his feelers" and see what he could find out.

Then I called Montana information and asked if there was an Agnes Embree in the Lame Deer area. "No. There's an Edward." I called and a chipper woman answered. Her husband Edward had died the year before at the age of 74. I told her I was looking for anyone related to a Jack Embree. She said her husband's father had been named Jack. I said Jack Embree had been married to a Northern Cheyenne woman named Agnes. There was a pause. "His mother's name was Agnes…but I'm pretty sure she wasn't Cheyenne." A different Jack and Agnes Embree?

Turns out that Agnes had died when Edward was 2 and Jack, of TB, when Edward was 15. He had been an orphan long before *my* Jack and Agnes were a part of this story. Then she said, "You know, I've always wanted to write down my father's story. He left home when he was 9 and became a hobo. Then he joined the carnival and wound up down in Cuba and drove a motorcycle in one of those drums until he cut off a man's head."

I asked for clarification, and she said he didn't actually cut off the man's head, but that there'd been an accident with the motorcycle and he'd sheared off the top of a man's skull, but that they wired a steel plate in place of the missing bone and the man had lived and actually become her father's good friend. After that, her father was in World War I, then became a bootlegger. I asked her where she lived, assuming it was near Lame Deer. She said she was outside Columbia Falls. Turns out she was about a mile from my closest friends in Montana. So we agreed to get together and talk when next I was up that way. A door had opened to another story but not the one I was after.

A week later I called Linwood Tall Bull again. He said that he had found out about a Greta Embree, not Agnes. But Greta had been on dialysis for some time and had died three months earlier. I was disappointed, but the passive side of my nature said, "You've done it again, chum – waited long enough for your chance to evaporate."

You were probably waiting for a payoff to what I've been telling you – I apologize. On the surface it does seem that all my trails are cold. That I *have* waited too long. Yes, I should have paid closer attention, I should have been more careful. The Powers-that-Be had entrusted me with information that I had not shown proper respect. Every one of us has experienced those instances of thinking, "If only I had asked her about..." But I know that the story is still there. In the white world, where we rely on writing everything down, stories do actually die out the same way that languages become extinct, that plant and animal species disappear. But in a culture based in the spoken word, a story, once told, becomes part of what Hindus call the Akhasic record – a record that includes everything that has ever been. The characters, whether dead or alive, are still there, waiting for someone to say the right word, to indicate they are worthy of receiving the story. In the white world we'd probably say case closed, but Indian time and Indian stories exist on a continuum which sometimes fades or goes underground until the right listener appears. I still have work to do. It will be harder, but I am finally listening. Whether I am worthy or not remains to be seen.

Talons

in memory of Sidney Keith

It was the third morning of the sundance. For me, this was
the fifth sundance I'd attended and the fourth here in this area
around Green Grass, South Dakota. The first two were spon-
sored by Arvol Looking Horse, Keeper of the Sacred Pipe
for the Lakota Nation, as part of his vision and commitment
to the Bigfoot Memorial Ride. For the second one of these
I'd brought along my son, who was 20 at the time and about
to enter his junior year of college. Arvol had set up the
grounds across the Moreau River and one had to drive across,
through the water, carefully, to get there. When we'd looked
around for a spot to set up our tent I'd found a good place a
little nearer the arbor than most of the tents and campers
which overlooked the river. Just as I started to throw down
our gear a young rattler gave me a warning: best heed it and
camp where the humans were congregated.

The sundance was followed by Arvol taking out the sacred pipe and performing a ceremony for upwards of 300
people. Probably 100 of those people were pipe carriers. I
was smoked out by the end of that event.

One ironic incident occurred the night of the fourth and
last day, after the feast and giveaway. Inipi lodges had been
set up, one for men, one for women. There were so many
men who wanted to sweat that there had to be three groups,
packed in three deep. I was in the last group. When it came
our turn, we waited and waited. The person supposed to be
leading our sweat was a sundancer, but we were told that he
had eaten too fast at the feast and was now suffering severe

cramps. What to do? A man stepped forward, in bikini un-
derwear, with a nipple ring and earrings, whose speech and
mannerisms were decidedly effeminate. He said that he was
Seneca and knew the songs and had led sweats before and
that he'd be willing to run things. The Lakota men, who tend
to be modest, were all wearing shorts but also had towels
wrapped around their waists, turned away – it was clear that
they wanted no part of this Seneca running the sweat. It was
considered bad form to wear metal in the sweatlodge, to boot.
One man spoke up and said they'd wait. The Seneca man
was clearly disgruntled at this rebuff, but he stayed. Traditional Lakota culture includes and honors men who are *winkte*.
The women are particularly accepting. But Lakota men can
be fairly macho and often avoid or spurn gays. Everyone stood
around uncomfortably until a substitute showed up to run
the sweat.

Then, last year, I'd attended the International Sundance,
conducted by Sidney Keith, who had taken it over from Frank
Fool's Crow some years ago. Sundances were starting to pro-
liferate around here. Someone had told me that there were as
many as eleven sundances going on at the same time within a
fifteen-mile radius of Green Grass. What would happen is
that someone would get a burr under their saddle about the
way So-and-So was running their sundance and form a splinter sundance of their own. The Pan-Indian movement had
accomplished much to ease inter-tribal bickering, but
differences of opinion and grudges on the intra-tribal level
were still an ingrained part of Indian life.

I was starting to recognize people and they were starting
to recognize me. The same elders were leading the sundance,
and Harry Charger, if he wasn't actually dancing or assist-
ing, was always around telling razor-sharp jokes. I'd recently
seen a photo of him in a piece on "The Buffalo" in *National*

Geographic, and when I brought it up, he said, "Yeah, I charged them double for that!" Then it dawned on me – the origin of his name. But no matter how much I opened up, I was still your basic misanthropic outsider. The previous night I'd actually broken away from my ascetic routine and gone into Eagle Butte with Gloria, a pretty Italian journalist, her son Daniele, and several others for dinner.

I slept in a pup tent on the periphery of the main enclave and boiled my water over a stick fire. I'd brought along nothing but apples and some packets of dehydrated soup, granola, powdered milk and tea bags. During this sundance as with the others I'd attended I did my best to dance under the arbor in support of the sundancers whenever they were dancing. And since they were fasting, I didn't think I should be frying up steaks or even brewing coffee within sniffing distance of them. In other words, I was attempting to honor their intentions and to focus my own attention on the sundance. Going into town for a steak dinner with Gloria and Daniele was a departure for me. Daniele was becoming like a nephew to me, which was in the spirit of the Lakota way. And Gloria, who knew more about the legal situation of Indians incarcerated in South Dakota than any South Dakotans, was always radiant. She was a sweetheart. And she always attracted a stray guy or two at every sundance, usually someone talented and good-looking but lonely. Seekers in that way, too. She treated everyone the same: with loving openness – easily misinterpreted. I think she was genuinely oblivious to the effect she had on men.

During the afternoon of the second day, a couple had set up camp near me in a sandy draw. They were Indian, probably Lakota. They parked their late model pickup and pitched a tent. The man was a big guy who kept his eyes down. And the woman was attractive but chunky. They were in their midthirties. After they'd settled in, the woman began to sing. I couldn't tell what she was singing because she sang quietly. I knew, though, that she wasn't singing sundance songs. The songs had a moaning quality to them. All I could tell was that they were in the Lakota language. She sang with her eyes closed, intently. After she was done, I walked by them on my way to the arbor and said hello as I passed. They both nodded slightly but neither looked up. There was something cold about them. Between the time they arrived and the time I left for dinner, they never set foot outside their camp and didn't interact with anyone. And even though they had a direct view of the sundance, never cast their eyes in that direction.

When our group returned from town, the man and woman were still there by themselves. They had a small fire going. I started one for tea. Just as it was getting dark, the woman sang again in that same way, secretively. I walked around and talked with a few people, came back, brushed my teeth, went a ways off, peed, then crawled into my tent. I don't remember anything unusual happening during the night. I was awakened once by a particularly baroque coyote serenade, with one pack trying to outdo another.

I woke just as the sun was rising. As I emerged from my tent I noticed that the man and woman were gone – no tent, no pickup. It was a clear day, going to be hot again. Sundances are scheduled throughout the summer, but this one usually took place early in August, when it's often 100 degrees with almost no humidity. I've heard of sundances taking place in the Seattle area, which makes no sense – the sun and the heat are supposed to make it a physical ordeal – how could that happen in Seattle's climate? The sundance was born on the plains. Some ceremonies are tied to their place of origin. This is one of them.

I boiled water. I had my powdered milk and granola in my tin cup, then my tea. I shaved, which I rarely did in civilian life, but always did, to be decorous, while at the sundance. Washed my cup and spoon, stowed them and proceeded toward the reeking, listing jerrybuilt port-a-john to take a dump. I took the long way around, detouring to where the couple had camped. Partially hidden in the grass was an object that caught my eye. I knelt and picked it up. What I found startled me to the point that I almost dropped it. It was a perfectly round stone, tannish in color, a little larger than a baseball, and glued to it were two severed eagle claws, as if they were grasping the stone. Why would they leave something like this? The day had been still except for the drumming and singing at the arbor but now the wind was rising. I took the object back to my tent and stuffed it into my sleeping bag.

By the time I went to the john and returned, it was getting windier. In the few times I'd been here, the weather, particularly during sundances, had been tied directly to the drama at hand. If we needed a spritz of rain to refresh the flagging dancers, a cloud would appear. If we needed a rainbow as a sign, there it was. If we needed it hotter, that's what we got. The weather and the place were one. Anyone who has witnessed a Hopi rain dance believes in these connections. We have the same idea in "Western" tradition, passed down from Hermes Trismegistus: "as above, so below" – the microcosm is a reflection of the macrocosm. You see it reflected, through neo-Platonism, in Shakespeare – the "Great Chain of Being." If we had been in Shakespeare's audience during a performance of *Julius Caesar* we would have known immediately that the quirky weather and other strange omens meant that Caesar should stay home the next day. In Lakota philosophy, life is a web, tying us all together: "If you do it unto the least of Mine, you do it unto Me." There have been several times I've seen the weather focus in directly on the sundance as if it were a conscious entity. And then there were other signs, too.

Once, down at Crow Dog's Paradise, on the Little White River, I climbed up a nearby hill and found myself being circled by ten eagles. I could hear their wings but they made no other sound.

The wind continued to pick up, coming from the south. I went to my tent to examine the object again. The claws were glued on so tightly that there would be no way of removing them intact. My tent was straining at its lines so I took it down and put it in my car. The blue tarps covering the arbor were flapping furiously, and people were standing on stepladders trying to lash them down. I could see concern on the faces of the dancers and everyone else there.

The drummers continued the steady heartbeat rhythm, singing in piercing eagle voices —

> *onsimala ye*
> *onsimala ye*
> *onsimala ye o ye o he*
> *oyate wakantanka he*
> *onsimala ye...*

I had a general idea what that meant – something like "Have pity on me...Have pity on the people...Great Mystery, have pity on me."

I sensed that I should help secure the tarps. I also thought that I should bring the rock to Sidney Keith and ask if it was important. But a kind of despair overcame me and all I wanted to do was get away from there as fast as I could. My intention had been to stay through the feast on the fourth day, but I threw my gear in the back and left, not even saying goodbye to Gloria and Daniele. I had the rock with me. I'd been walking out all my life, so this was nothing new, but my soul felt sour and cheapened.

By the time I had passed the Dairy Queen in Eagle Butte heading west, the winds had fallen off. I was on my way to Bozeman, to do some hiking, see old friends, let off steam.

This was the only time of year I could get away from my job for more than a weekend, and fortunately it coincided with the sundance. It also fell during the Harley "event" in Sturgis. I always stopped there, looked around, bought a tee-shirt out of solidarity – but had no real interest in the vibe. This year, as I cruised the main drag I noticed that there was an AA meeting set up just for bikers. There were the usual halter-tops and tight pants on the biker chicks, some of them foxes, some of them dogs. At the edge of town I saw a huge crane from which 300-pound lard-asses were bungee jumping.

*

The idea that life is a web certainly applied to my life in Bozeman. I'd left behind connections many of which were rich and ongoing, several incomplete. That was the backdrop, in perpetuity, of my visits. I was staying with my friends Dan and Bette, who had offered me, for some years, the use of their downstairs guest bedroom. I showed them the rock with claws attached and the three of us speculated feebly about its meaning.

That afternoon I bought two different USGS maps of the Bridgers, the range which borders Bozeman's Gallatin Valley on the east. I'd always wanted to walk the length of the Bridgers. I knew there was a footrace every year in which a gang of maniacs followed the same route I was planning – ascending Sacajawea from Fairy Lake then just sticking to the ridge until it came out above the "M" across from the fish hatchery. I was plump but in decent shape for a man of my age and sedentary lifestyle, but not out to break any records. Dan agreed to drive me to Fairy Lake the next morning.

Before sun-up I checked my knapsack – two water bottles, three granola bars, a few squares of toilet paper, an extra pair of socks and my poncho – I was set. I'd wear shorts, a tee-shirt, cotton socks and my hiking boots. Dan was already up, had put out cereal and brewed coffee. Dan and Bette were my safe haven from the psychological briar patch I'd left in Bozeman.

As we were driving out Bridger Canyon, which was starting to get Californicated like the rest of the area, I saw many houses, ranches, rock formations and ridges which brought back powerful associations. This is where I'd had my first serious relationship, my first child had been born, and I'd had my first real job. But I'd arrived in 1970, when the times they were still very much a changin'. Even now, over twenty years later, I had a tendency to plummet into my memories and wallow.

We passed a cabin where I used to hole up, a house where I had been to dinner several times, then the ski slope, Bridger Bowl. Never had much use for downhill – couldn't afford it and didn't like the atmosphere. The sun was just coming up as we turned off the main road up toward Fairy Lake. As we approached the parking area Dan asked me when I thought I'd get back from this hike. I told him that it seemed like maybe an eight-hour leisurely walk – to expect me before dark. When we got out and I shouldered my knapsack he said, "If you're not back by morning I'm going to send the rescue crew in after you." He wasn't joking. Dan wasn't a hiker himself, but he knew I often underestimated times and distances and just as frequently pushed my own limits. I scanned Fairy Lake – had I been Thoreau, this would have been my Walden – minus the day-campers, of course. We hugged each other and I started up the switchbacks of Sacajawea.

On the way up, I was reminded of that famous photo of the string of miners heading up Chilcoot Pass into the goldfields of the Yukon. I picked some small wild onions to supplement my bland breakfast – they were so sweet. At the top I paused to decide whether to stay on the ridge or drop down to a more inviting game trail. I chose the latter. I knew that people used this area for hang gliding. It would be great to see the landscape from that vantage but I knew I couldn't face the prospect of hurtling to the earth like Icarus. There was still snow in ravines that didn't get much sun. At the edge of one I encountered the familiar musk of death – the decomposing body of a mule deer that had died during the winter. I was making good time but, as usual in the mountains, not as fast as the map would have me believe.

The good thing about this ridge route is that you always have the Gallatin Valley to the west to give you your bearings. It was heating up and I was getting worn out side-hilling as the trail appeared and disappeared. This was going to take longer than I expected, but I could still make it down by dark. Then I noticed that one of my water containers had slipped out of my knapsack. I had passed the point at which I could drop down to Bridger Bowl and thumb to town through Bridger Canyon so I had to push on. I looked west and figured I was just past Bostwick Creek Canyon. I was using a stick I'd broken off a dead tree to help steady myself but in one rocky patch I slipped and narrowly avoided impaling myself on the sharp end. That would be a stupid way to go. Keep your wits about you, sayeth the Inner Guide.

I didn't have a watch but I knew it was getting toward evening. I drank my last two swallows of water. I was approaching Bridger Peak when the sky darkened suddenly and a storm came blowing in from the west. I was on a ledge about three feet wide when hailstones the size of gobstoppers started nailing me. I hunkered down and took out my poncho – my only protection. I was getting hammered but it would be too treacherous to move forward – a sheer drop off if I slipped. This should pass quickly.

But the hail was followed immediately by very high winds, which were blowing stinging rain in at me almost horizontally. Despite my poncho, I was drenched.

When the rain finally let up it was dark, except for the lights of ranches out in the valley. The thin moon was hidden behind scudding clouds. I could edge ahead and get off this ledge one step at a time but now it was pitch dark and everything was slick and one false step and it would be all over. I decided to wait out the night on the ledge. As I said, I was wearing shorts, a tee-shirt, socks and hiking boots, which were now sopping wet. I bunched up in my poncho in a fetal position and tried to sleep. But my teeth were chattering. The wind had dropped off somewhat but it was still gusting. I meditated distractedly and chanted to pass the time and eventually was able to sleep for short bursts until either my fear of rolling off the ledge woke me or the condensation on the inside of the poncho brought on another bout of the shivers. And then there was more stinging rain. I didn't think about much during the night except that I'd told Dan I'd be back by dark and that he and Bette would be worried. And that if I'd gotten past this ledge I might have been able to keep going. Might.

False dawn arrived and I could see well enough to work my way along the ledge and on toward Baldy. My legs were leaden and all my water gone. I stumbled along and finally got to the point where I was descending – going down is always harder on the feet and legs than going up. I came across a hiker who was surprised to see me. He told me that the rescue squad was looking for a guy. I told him that that would probably be me. I told him that I hadn't had any water since early evening, and about having to spend the night on the ledge. He handed me a canteen and said I could have what I needed but to leave some for him – it was "going to be a scorcher." He was sizing me up, wondering how I could have gotten myself into that kind of fix.

I continued down the slope. Usually I half-run down stretches like this, but my feet were too beat up for that. After several hours I came out above the "m" (for Montana State University) and could see a horse trailer, a horse, and two men down in the parking area. I picked up my pace. It was Dan and one of the rescue guys.

When I reached them Dan came forward and hugged me then kissed my forehead and said, "We thought we'd lost you, buddy. I waited until 9 this morning then I called the rescue unit."

The rescue guy told me that if I hadn't shown up when I did they would have come in looking for me. They had two other men on horseback who were ready to go in from Bridger Bowl. He radioed headquarters and called off the search. Dan gave me a lukewarm Coke, which I guzzled down. The rescue guy told me that I was required to come in to the office to give them a report of what had happened. I went home with Dan and splashed some water on my face then to the office to make my report. I met with three men. They offered me coffee and were quite cordial – I had expected them to be hard-asses about it. They had their maps out and asked me detailed questions. It was clear that they wanted as much specific information out of me as they could get, to aid them in future rescues. They even asked me what I thought were the best ways in to that spot. As I was leaving their office I noticed that the back of my shorts was split wide open and I'd been walking around with my ass hanging out. Literally as well as figuratively.

I had to get on the road that evening to be back at work the morning after next. I went back to Dan and Bette's and took a long shower then drank a beer. I don't drink beer any more, but that's what I needed. As I was packing I felt the heft of the strange stone. Maybe I should wear it around my neck like an albatross. Why hadn't I brought it to Sidney Keith? What was I going to do with it now? Whatever it was, I had to get it out of my hands.

I said goodbye to Dan and Bette and made good time through Wyoming and into South Dakota. Near Rapid City I went south toward Chadron, Nebraska. Exhausted, I pulled off Highway 20, a two-lane, near Hay Springs, to sleep for a few hours. It was 2 AM. I found a nice grove of cottonwoods down a farm lane. I could hear cattle ruminating in a pasture nearby. I slept fast and deep.

When I awoke, I noticed that my ankles had swollen considerably – the hike had taken more out of my body than I'd figured – not as resilient as in my prime. My feet were still functional – I'd have to make sure to stop and walk around every hour or so. It was a little dewy this morning. I conversed with the Angus bull in the pasture then turned back on to the main road. With the dew in the morning sun, there was a jewel on every blade of grass – as if everything had gold wings. If I were a painter of landscapes, there would be an unlimited supply of subjects right here. Each farm road wound through to the horizon in the most perfect way, the palate of colors intricately subtle.

I took 250 south through the Sand Hills, then east on 20. I had a spectacular traditional roast beef Sunday lunch in Hyannis, but otherwise my return to Iowa City was uneventful. The round stone with claws attached was wrapped in a towel in my knapsack.

*

Two weeks later I went over to have dinner with my friend LeAnne, a Choctaw from Oklahoma, and her husband Jim, who'd grown up outside Iowa City. His parents had the best apple orchard in the area. Jim was quiet and thoughtful, LeAnne, a hell-raiser and a hell of a writer. I had told her I wanted her opinion about something, so she said to come over for dinner. Their apartment was more like a small museum than a dwelling – every inch of the walls was covered with photos and objects related to their travels or their relatives. Floor space, the same. It was going to be chili for dinner, hot hot chili. Jim cooking.

LeAnne asked me what I wanted an opinion about. I went to the car and returned with the rock and claws. When she saw it, she backed away and said, "I don't know what it is or what it means, but it is evil – get it out of here! I don't want to touch it."

Shortly after that I took several photographs of it and sent them to Sidney Keith with a letter explaining where I had found it and when, and about being trapped in the Bridgers. I also told him about LeAnne's reaction to it. I wanted to know whether it was in some way a sacred object and whether I should return it to him. I got a letter back that said the following:

Dear Mr. McCullough:

Thank you for your letter. I have looked over your photographs carefully and can tell you exactly what you have. When our people won the lawsuit and received millions of dollars for the Black Hills, the tribal council decided to keep the money in the bank to let it draw interest. I suspect the government assumed we'd take the money and divide it. There is a small group that wants to distribute the money right now, and they have been using witchcraft to try to undermine traditional ceremonies. What you have was brought to the sundance by the couple you saw who were part of this group. The round stone represents the Black Hills and the eagle claws cut off like that are a kind of left-handed power symbol. The eagle is powerful but they are using its power the wrong way. The strong wind we experienced that day was a direct result of that stone being at the sundance. You were the one chosen to remove it. The winds stopped completely after half an hour, or just after you left, according to what you told me. Your experience in the mountains happened because you still had the stone and the powers of evil wanted to punish you. Do not send me the stone. It is not sacred. You should take it out somewhere and bury it. If you do that it will no longer have any power over you or anyone else.

Sincerely,
Sidney Keith

The next day, one of those crisp fall football Saturdays, I got in the car and drove around until I found a small country cemetery. I went out beyond the trees where no one could see me from the road and dug down some three feet and dropped the stone into its grave. Hopefully, Sidney Keith knows what he is talking about – that it will be permanently out of commission, no longer having influence even over the spirits of those buried near it, or if someone unearths it inadvertently at some point in the future – it is not just waiting down there like a land mine.

How The Crazy Dog Society Came to Be

One night, in the moon of ponies' shedding, a skinny man with a big mole on his left cheek lay down to sleep in the sand rocks. He was up above the village in the place where the coyotes make their trilling. In his dream that night, it was dawn and the ponies' tails were tied up as if a fight were coming, and the river's voice could not be heard beneath the ice. The shadows of the clouds hurried across the ponies as the warriors tied charms in their manes and painted hail on their rumps. The skinny man saw himself riding back and forth, yipping to his brothers, tapping at them with his quirt. In the world outside this dream he had counted coup but once. He awoke and kept this dream to himself, thinking it may have been a story told him by his grandfather.

The next night he slept in the same place and had the same dream, but now he saw different charms in the ponies' manes, the swifthawk tied in his uncle's hair, the words of the exhortations from his own mouth.

The next night he dreamed it deeper, and the fourth night he saw it from his own eyes, looking out.

That next morning he awoke and walked tall to the village. The air was still, the smoke straight up in gray plumes. He built up a fire and called his brothers to tell them of his dream. They just nodded and swatted at the slow-moving flies. He had never been one to speak his mind, but now his voice was deep with knowing. He chose four from among them and told them to bring his dream to the Keeper of the Sacred Arrows. They were reluctant, but did it because he was their brother.

The keeper was a short man with big arms and a strong chin beneath his steady eyes, which looked right through people to the truth. His wife had died and he lived alone, smiling only when he danced. The four chosen told the keeper that their skinny brother had had a medicine dream and wished to start a new society of warriors.

The keeper listened to their words, looking through them at something in the distance. Finally he spoke. One word, "No." And shooed them from his lodge.

When the skinny man was told this he held his head and made a crying sound. But that night he danced around the fire, crying that he would make the keeper see the power of his dream.

When morning came, the camp was silent. It was too silent. When the people left their lodges they saw that there were no dogs about the camp. No puppies chasing tails, no big dogs growling over the legbone of an antelope, or barking just to keep in practice. The skinny man's fire still smoldered but he was gone. They noticed this, but did not think it odd.

When the sun was up above the trees, the hunters went to look for game. One of the strongheart men was first to see it on a hillside as he rode beyond the trees. The skinny man stood in silhouette on the crest of a large hill, and all around were dogs, hundreds of them, maybe a thousand. The hunter saw his own dog among them, and others from the village. The skinny man stood with palms extended to the sun. There were dogs of every size and shape all curled there, peaceful in the sun at the feet of the skinny man, even one coyote.

The hunter saw another hunter come from the trees and stop to look at this. They signaled each other and rode fast back to the village to tell the keeper. The keeper heard their words and now more men had seen it and the people of the village stood around talking of the dogs.

Then, when the sun was overhead, the skinny man returned. He came to the keeper's lodge and asked to enter. The keeper welcomed him and told the skinny man that his vision was indeed true, and he gave his blessing on this new society of warriors. Then they both heard loud voices from outside. When they looked out, they saw a long line of dogs coming down the hill in single file; the keeper's dog was first in line. The dogs hopped the apron of the lodge through the door the keeper held for them and walked, in single file, around the lodge, from left to right, as the sun moves, stopping to sniff the sacred bundle of the arrows. They were silent, knowing, not as dogs behave. When they hopped back outside, they returned to the ways of dogs, racing around and nipping and sniffing, and the strays ran off with each other. The people in the village all laughed at this spectacle.

And there was a big dance that night, honoring the skinny man and his vision. And so it was that the Crazy Dog Society came to be.

based on the Northern Cheyenne story
as told by John Wooden Legs, 1974
in Bozeman, Montana

Diamonds

I met my great-grandfather, David Shallcross Yould, only once, when he was 92 and I was 9. He had come down from Canada to see Game Three of the '52 World Series between the Yankees and the Dodgers. More specifically, he was there to see his hero, Jackie Robinson. His visit coincided with one of my family's visits to my grandmother's house in Staten Island.

My great-grandfather was born in 1860 and had lived all his life in Nova Scotia. He had been a railroad engineer on the Canadian Pacific Railway until his retirement. I remember seeing a sepia-toned photograph of him standing next to a huge steam engine with his usual bemused and confident expression. I remember, also, hearing that he had been the engineer (or one of them) on the first Trans-Canada run, although I've not been able to corroborate this – he would have been in his mid-20s at that time. He was a big man, or seemed so to me, just over 6 feet, with a barrel chest, and wore his pants high, held up with suspenders. He had a cocky smile. He lived to be 93 and my great-grandmother to 91. In a photograph of them on their 75th wedding anniversary she appears frail by comparison. The backyard of their narrow clapboard Truro home was chockablock with huge flowers. I always attributed their longevity to the slow pace of life in Nova Scotia, the absence of stress. Genetics was clearly a factor, too – my great-grandfather's cousin Harry lived to be 106.

Naturally, when my great-grandfather traveled to New York, he took the train from Halifax to Grand Central. When he arrived at my grandmother's house on St. Paul's Avenue, he stepped out of my Uncle Bill's car and shook hands with me and my cousin Billy, beaming that broad smile on us. He had a worn baseball mitt under his arm, which looked to be of Ty Cobb vintage. He asked us if we wanted to play catch; we scrambled into the house to get our mitts. We lobbed the ball back and forth with him on the uneven gray flagstone sidewalk for about forty-five minutes.

That must have been October 1st. My Uncle Dave, who was a big shot with TWA , had gotten him a seat in the TWA box for the game on the 3rd, in Yankee Stadium – there was no TWA box in Ebbets Field.

My dad was a career NCO in the U.S. Air Force, so our family was frequently on the move. We had been stationed in Newfoundland, and would return there for another tour after a year in San Bernardino. My own obsession with baseball had yet to begin; I had no idea who Jackie Robinson was. I'd been born in Staten Island but never really lived there except for half of second grade, and half of fourth grade to come. Most of the other boys my age divided into Yankee, Dodger and Giant camps, and often came to blows over these allegiances. I was oblivious. I remember my Uncle Bill, who was a Yankee fan, saying that Robinson "could beat you with a bunt, a homer, or a stolen base." Over his 10-year career he stole home 19 times, five in one year. I knew nothing then of his remarkable rookie season in '47 when he broke the color barrier, or his MVP in '49, or the six pennants in ten years. He was just a name to me.

My Uncle Dave escorted my great-grandfather to the game on October 3rd, a perfect fall day. The Dodgers won that game 5–3 but lost the Series four games to three. Robinson had had a good but not sensational year, and his Series performance was lackluster: he batted only . 174, with 4 hits in 23 at-bats, one homer and two RBI's. But in that game, with the Dodgers hanging on to a one-run lead in the top of the 9th, Reese and Robinson had both singled, moved around on a double steal, and scored on a passed ball. Mize homered for the Yanks in the bottom of the 9th, but Preacher Roe held on to win it. My great-grandfather and 66,697 other fans had seen vintage Robinson.

Two days later a photograph appeared in the *Staten Island Advance* with the headline RAIROAD ENGINEER MEETS HIS HERO. There, in the photograph, was David Yould, of Truro, Nova Scotia, arm-in-arm with Jackie Robinson, both of them smiling broadly. The caption went on to say that Mr. Yould had made the trip from Canada to see Robinson play because he regarded him as his personal hero.

My great-grandfather died in April of the following year, quietly, in his sleep. They said he had a smile on his face. Robinson retired in '56 and died at the age of 53, gray and tired from his struggles on the field and in the field of civil rights.

I never had a chance to ask my great-grandfather about that day, or to find out any more specifics about his regard for Jackie Robinson. I don't even know whether he'd been a baseball player himself. No one in the family has a copy of that yellowed newspaper clipping and my search of the *Staten Island Advance* archives was a bust. But the image of those two smiling men, arm-in-arm, at ease in each other's presence, is as clear as the day I first saw it more than half a century ago.

Memories of An Air Force Batboy
Upper Peninsula, Michigan
Late Fifties

CARL BELFATTI

Carl Belfatti, righthander from Philly, fit his name – he was a beautiful fat man. His fastball dipped like a barn swallow. He'd jam righthanders with his inshoot, breaking off the bats in their hands – at least three a game when he was hot. The only guy who could hit him was Moose, an old steelmill hand from the Soo who was built like Grover Cleveland. Moose's swing was Kluszewskian – the ball would rocket into the parking lot and even took out the base commander's El Dorado windshield once. Belfatti bowled a perfect game on the alley next to mine. Scouts from the Yankees wanted to sign him when his hitch was up. Carl told me to hit one guy a game – to never go for the head, but go at their best hitter so that he'll never have a chance to dodge it. I did that, scowling in with a three-day Maglie stubble.

NICK PREDOVIC

Nick Predovic took a two-step walking lead. He was 39 when he joined the team, time in the Pacific Coast League, busted down repeatedly but up again to Tech Sergeant. Leather vocabulary written in his eyes, cracked croak from two packs of Luckies every day. 6 foot 1, 185, he was the Hoover of

third basemen, and the second looey playing first took to
wearing sponges in his glove. Two steps slower than in his
prime he could still steal second on any southpaw and make
any catcher's rifle arm seem like blowing smoke. Back before
the head-first and the drive-by slide Predovic could adjust his
hook to the body language of the baseman covering the bag,
spikes high if need be. Third especially a breeze for him –
he'd have it made while the pitcher was shaking off the second sign. He'd taunt them like a foul-mouthed mockingbird.
I was there for two seasons and never saw him cut down once
despite their pitchouts, their pickoff afterthoughts. He was
our scarred mongoose, bane of many cobras. I learned that
rhythm from him, that ruthlessness of when to strike.

JIM PARKER

Jim Parker, Willacoochie, Georgia – red-haired, crewcut,
pockmarks on his neck. Gentleman Jim: "Yes-sir, no-sir, yes
ma'am…" Taught me how to fold my cap: a high ridge in
front, lower in the back, accordion-style, wet it down and put
a rubber band around the skinny end of the wedge until it
dries – pure sex – like spit-shined brogans or that crooked
Elvis smile I'd practice in the mirror. Parker taught me how
to change my speeds, and different ways to use the seams. His
delivery was over the top, like Koufax. He was a stud, a show-
man, a true ace.

PETE KOOSKALIS

Pete Kooskalis was the prince of malice. From South Boston,
he spoke what he called "The King's English." His words

were blue, dark blue, Prussian blue. He told that one-armed ump to "Take a flying fuck at the moon," and when we played a Canuck team on their home turf he told their catcher to "Go fuck the Queen." Their entire bench emptied as did ours, bats in hand. Never knew Canadians cared that much for the Queen. Pete was our version of Billy Martin, at second base, at the plate, on the road. Back in civilian life, I left my teen-age teammates slack-jawed when I'd pepper them with the blue epithets I learned from Pete.

MURPH, ETC.

Murphy, a Sgt. Major, was the coach. Had that crusty Frank Lovejoy smile and if he didn't have a tattoo it was because he didn't need one. Permanent tan and those squinty Roy Rogers eyes, with that "cross-me-boy-and-you're-dead-meat-just-do-your-job-and-we'll-get-on-fine" look. He'd let me pitch batting practice until I'd try a crossfire and plunk someone. I'd be humming it in there, having visions of being called up at 17 like Bobby Feller, or 15 like Nuxey.

In May, my dad got me on a Babe Ruth team in the Soo, forty miles away, a long commute. The day of my first game my grandma died; they put him on a flight that afternoon. He'd asked me how I'd get up to the game and I'd said I'd hitchhike from the highway. On his way to the flightline, he saw me playing catch with Don Prince and Steve Haywood. He veered over and asked me what I was doing; I told him it was too far to hitchhike. He set his jaw and told me to get in. He missed his mother's funeral to get me there.

That summer I struck out 17 in a seven-inning game, pitched a one-hitter in another, and led the league in batting. The seventeen strikeouts in a morning game after which I had three root beer floats and four hotdogs, caught the second game and went five-for-five, with eight ribbies. Dad got Don and Steve on the team, too, and all three of us made the All-Stars. They took us out after just two innings, we were so far ahead of those pint-sized Canucks. Don and Steve were both close to 6 feet – the opposing manager asked to see our birth certificates.

On a family outing to Lake Michigan I went back to the car to jack off and fantasize about Bessie Brierly or her dark Costa Rican mother who did a wild rhumba down at the NCO Club – at least in my fantasy. And heard the second half of Bunning's no-hitter in George Kell's pre-Harwellian drone. It was the summer I saw Ted Williams for the first time, on the tube, the All-Star Game. In our double-header the next night, every hitter worth his salt mimicked The Splinter to his minutest nuance.

It seems I peaked early; the rest caught up.

I'd come home after dark always, my dinner wrapped in foil in the oven, and the TV news from the Soo: "Blast Furnace 52-Finishing Mill 49…" The summer, after a hot shower, I tried to cure my jock itch with wintergreen oil, the summer of father-son tension, the summer I planned to run away from home in the flat scrub Upper Peninsula, but there were wolves and who'd ever find me, and then who'd feel sorry. Summer of *Bird Dog, Purple People Eater, Lonesome Town* and *Yellow Polkadot Bikini,* of pegged pants, thin white belts, of looking down bathing suits, of ramrod boners. Some general's daughter had the hots for me and even had the bulldog hood ornament from a Mack truck on her dresser in my honor. But I was told "not to go there," that it was "inappropriate" to spark a general's daughter.

How I Got My Summer Vaccination

In the summer of my sixteenth year I lived in my overcoat half the day studying geometry and tectonic deuteronomy and blonde girls with high heels and asses. I took classes in typing blood and other body fluids and played baseball in a baseball suit the rest of the time I wasn't holding up the centerpole of the universe. And one time when the nighthawks wouldn't let me sleep and lifting the weight of the world wasn't enough I took a job at a circus. The circuses came and went and I set them up and tore them down. Carousel parts, Chinese red and thickly greased, gears for engines of torture from Bunyan's nightmares. Mildewed canvases, men with cigars, everything smelling of piss, despair and resignation. Objects constantly impaled my palms – filaments of giant bulbs, nails, blades of light spinning out of septic darkness. And the women waited in every shadow, painted designs on my chest and pressed against me. And the fat woman emerged from her trailer every night the same to feed her chihuahua whose front legs had been sawed off and she'd offer it some raw tidbit and its eyes would bug and it would tilt toward the plastic dish until she'd yank the dish away and the little wretch would topple forward on its face and kick its back legs like a frog and a round phlegmish laugh would roll out from her and she'd roll her eyes, thrust her hidden crotch at me, spewing red beans and rice. But in all those blackstrap nights my eyes never once left her face.

Suitland, Maryland
1959

122

Kit Miller's Tale

in memory of Kathryn Cosgriff Miller
(April 21, 1908–May 23, 1982)

The wind tells me I am in Valhalla. A magpie leaps from behind a cedar and tells me this is Bozeman – Montana – the
veterans' section of the boneyard. This watchbird heckles me
until I find *your* stone next to Earl's, your husband. KIT in one
corner, POET in the other – a mean memorial. So this is where
time turned you on your head and your heart finally filled
with sand.

> It's me again, Kit, my grave mood in tow.
> The wind says I'm at an all-time low.
> The wind says it's time for me to go.
> The stunted cedars lean in to hear
> a French horn, a concertina, and an
> Irish drum, so why so glum, chum?
> Or is it just tinnitus behind my eardrum
> or the tinkling of a tintinabulum?

The first time I've showed up to visit.

Here is the crushed and odoriferous Gauloise I mooched
from a famous novelist last night at the Crystal Bar – he was
a connoisseur of fishing gear and bearshit – I light it up. I still
don't smoke these days but it was free and this is in your honor.
Smells like the shirt of a sweaty voyageur.

Next time I'll bring a bottle of something good, muster
out what's left of the old guard. We'll dig you up and set

your bones in a chair – you'll get time off for leprechaun behavior. *Oh, wind, you've played me, taken everything.* You see,
Kit – after all these years I'm still rehearsing – Imposter! Po-
seur! Who never got it off the ground. But with you around,
I believed – in Celtic flourishes, in our chivalric code.

*

I remember first meeting you in the fall of '70. That first
week of my first year teaching, a short round woman came
up after class to ask if she could listen in. Lavender pants suit,
large eyes with the cast of one half crazed, but in on the cosmic joke. I observed you sometimes laughed at nothing; you
couldn't seem to help it – while all the rest of us worked hard
at being tragic.

After you had checked me out you asked if I would help
you start a renegade poets' group: "No bluehairs who write
about buffalo skulls, wagon wheels, and bind their books in
birch bark." Our menagerie ran the age and persuasion gamut
– Fellini tinged with Bergman – nonetheless, our work and
lives grew deeper with our friendship.

Remember when we filled a washtub up with gin and several kinds of fruit juice, then you passed out lengths of plastic tubing, then Deb danced on your kitchen table? – She was
Betty Grable with cellulite. At parties, you were always last
to fold, saying, at the end, "Watchman, what of the night?"
You told me it was what you used to say when you'd pass the
whores' cribs along the creek each night on your way home
from Deaconess back when you worked grave shift as a nurse.

Since you'd been raised a hardcore Mick I thought it a
breakthrough that you latched onto the Methodists up the
block who sang Neil Diamond songs as hymns. And you'd
borrow Buddhist texts from me – no one mistook you for a

New Age mystic, but remember that famous night when you picked up the local country-western radio station loud and clear on the tinfoil round your geranium? Cowboy Copas, if I recall correctly. And you told us it wasn't the *first* time.

You never talked much about growing up in that one-room cabin north of Graycliff with eleven siblings, but whenever our group would plan some private retreat, you'd say, "Sorry, friends, *I'll* stick with *in*door plumbing!"

When June went down in public with a stroke, when Julie's pet rat had a heart attack and bellied up during Christmas dinner, when all our lives unwound, you'd nurse us back.

Once, I was between lives; you put me up in you sons' room. I felt just like your son, your nephew, in some odd way, your lover – a "younger man," forty years your junior. *That* would have caused a scandal!

Don't know how much you hear up here – your son Rocque, the architect, maintains a monkish life in easy isolation. Tommy, the older one, is dead now – never seemed to recover from Vietnam. My guess is he favored Earl, while Rocque took after you. Anne, your only sibling to outlive you, lives alone in Whitehall and still has several bones to pick with you.

*

I left town when the well went dry for me. But I kept tabs on you up to the very end. I heard tell that you took your grandma act anywhere there was a cause worth fighting. And it always worked, you shifty thing! And you kept writing poems. I heard about the time a high school teacher had you in and asked you what you thought of her personal favorite, Robert Frost. You said he had four good poems at the max, that the kids should read the poets with *cajones*. I suspect you copped *that* attitude from me. As time has passed I've come to see the many virtues of his work. And you?

After you left town and went to live with Tommy, Sue, and your grandkids, I saw you just that once, when I was in San Jose visiting my son. As the three of us walked, we found a sparrow lying in the street, and revived it. You were still a wide-eyed, happy conspirator. When I heard you died I grieved, not bitterly, but with a smile.

I've yet to *become* Robert Frost, but I did take his "road less traveled by," and came to yet another fork – a rutted track through wilderness; I could find no signs, no blazes – sometimes it even disappeared. Now and then I'd get off the trail to bushwhack, but would go back to watch the main road through the trees. I've drifted, not like you, my friend. Whenever I've let my mind go I've seen you, Kit, at a distance, but have yet to catch your eye. You have gotten what you deserved, I have gotten what I wanted but not the way I wanted it.

Yeats, your favorite, said "we're forced to choose perfection of the life or of the work" – thinking I could master both, I've chosen neither.

*

You should get out and take a look around – since your demise they've built another mall, mostly Pataguccians moving in these days and investment brokers – gentilhommes, come to angle in the streams. The Oaks is now an upscale health food store. Don't know where they've sent the regulars – always feared I'd end up spitting blood in a room at the Range Hotel – knock on wooden head.

How long has it been, dear Katie Cosgriff? I feel like Rip Van Winkle, but these days round these parts, I'm apt to be Rip Torn. Up, Santa Fe! Boulder! Up! Sedona!

Whose guffaw? Is that you, Kit, or am I just rambling to myself? Is this another gag, Kit, a set-up? I don't expect to see you face to face until some snowbound night in April when I push that heavy door ajar to find you at the right hand of the lord as he swipes the foam from his big red beard and rumbles at your jokes. You'll wink at me.

But now that crusty wind speaks up again.

> Kit, I've got to beat it out of here;
> the killing frost has touched my hair,
> and things I once did on a dare
> are whispers on the wind.

> You won't hear from me again
> until my own clock's striking ten;
> I will have learned my lines by then.
> I'll stand here singing to these stones
> and coax the laughter from your bones.

Last Ditch

for Bill Bode

Cold morning out on the pipeline, welder putting on a patch.
I slip off to take a shit – torn clouds tumble over dry corn.
Inside the fence, Angus steers, eyes wide, roll wild in steamy
upturned earth from backhoe: bovine catnip. Side boom clat-
ters by – full joint and a pup in tow. In the trench, Joe strings
his bead, flips hood down to make a hot pass. Martin snoring
in his pickup, sweating out three quarts of Mad Dog, swill
brandy on the side.

   News today: – "Teamster bellies up one and a quarter"
   – "The boom hand from Lemoni had the clap – passed it
      on to that gal from Tipton *as well as* her daughter"
   – "That one Lacey was with last night was so old her pussy
      hair was wore off – her teeth was on the night table
      when I come in – but he said her gums was sure soft"
   – "If that cockamamie inspector don't figger his ass out
      soon, we'll backfill right over him"
Bodell bagged two cocks on the way from his house – our
lunch today, served from his tailgate. I wipe off with brittle
corn leaves.

   Yesterday, on the pipetruck, kid had two fingers mashed
off 'tween two pipes – made me goosey. I see I ain't no cowboy: *the last roundup*, sez he. When I drag up, Joe will push
back his polkadots, spit a stream of Redman, and say, "Yeah,
he was a okay hand, alright…for that type."

Down Point

for Jack Roundy

I rose from a grove of scrub oak, at the thick of the planet, on a point of land, in a cove near Bath, Maine. It was the last leg of August. I thought the tent was burning – just the woodsmoke in my clothes. I could hear the morning tide.

Up the hill, your uncle's pipe was glowing on the porch. He could not live on in town where none were self-sufficient – he preferred to be down point. The six of us had set up camp within coughing distance from him, loaves and fishes wrapped in foil.

*

Schlump out in black slime the consistency and stench of sewage. The rotted boots they've lent me will not stay on my feet so I wear my old (and only) running shoes. Slock the short rake hard into the muck just ahead of a puny spout of water. Pull back the mud and try to discern which one I dredge up still has a "smoking gun." Hold it aloft for the watchers on the shore – this must be a joke they share with Squanto, who hoodwinked their forebears into doing this. Pitch the creature into a crusty hod. Slap at midges and coat my legs with mud, which attracts them even more – after all, it's the same filth they live in. Slock again – this time uncover a foot-long seaworm, pink and gristly as a fresh intestine. Bosch, behold! Acres of putrid detritus peopled with monsters from my darkest dreams. Fill hod with clams between stings from midges – throw in a few I know are mudders to inflate the body count.

*

The fog sinks down in the trees. A blue heron cranes its neck on a perch and waits, stock-still. Lobsters with bands on their claws drift in a murky bucket. We have fired the cauldron. We drop them in, one by one. Their color changes, and the life bleeds out into night air. On the grill, we steam our clams. I crack one open and the smell of heavy sex fills my hands.

Father's Day, 1990

My son is home for the weekend, sporting his freshman soc-
cer mullet. We are canoeing up a slough I used to walk in my
glory days, when he spots a foundering Angus calf. Two
turtles croak at us from a sodden trunk as we beach where
the cattle come down to drink. The calf is jumpy, unused to
human contact. I try to herd it up the flowered hillside to
find its mother. I tell my son the calf seems shaky, maybe it is
sick, abandoned by the herd. By now it is docile and responds
to my touch. I send my son to see if he can turn the herd
back this way. In a few minutes I can hear bellowing and
bawling from over the hill.

The calf's breathing is shallow, and there is milky slob-
ber hanging from its muzzle. As it steps down into a ditch
leading to the herd's shady spot under some oaks, the calf
collapses.

My son's voice comes from the crest of the hill. He ap-
proaches: "The herd was too goosey. There were bulls out
there... looked as if they might charge." He kneels to look
the calf over, shakes his head. I say we'd best get it out of
the sun.

"Will it bite?" he asks.

"Too weak," I tell him.

I take the front legs in one hand and support the lolling
head with the other; he takes the hind legs. We shuffle over
to a sprawling sycamore, which will give shade until the sun
sets. The left eye, facing us, begins to roll back and the calf
breathes in fits and starts.

"There was no sign of any farmhouse," my son says.

It makes no sense to put the calf in our canoe since we must portage around the dam. It wouldn't last that long, anyway. And if it started to revive, capsizing us as we approached the spillway, what then?

PLOT FOILED! HIPPIES TRY TO RUSTLE BY CANOE

We stroke the calf's head and ears and talk to it. Finally we say some words over its dwindling life, asking the cosmos to spiral down and take up its sweet soul. Then we walk away.

"Our yearly lesson in mortality," my son says. I don't need to look at him to know the expression on his face. There are five friends buried in our yard – three of them (two cats and a dog) died of old age as we held them in our arms. The other two were newborn mice. When his dog Rhubarb died, my son said, "He was the only constant in my life."

Later, when we're driving back to pick up my son's car we both realize we could have brought the squirt bottle up from the canoe. But the calf had been standing right next to the water when we'd first seen it. And it would have been easy enough for me to sling the calf across my shoulders and carry it back to the herd.

At dinner that night, my son says he's seen a movie in which Egyptians suck out the brains of their dead through a tube. I remember touching my father's empty skull, there in his coffin. I was 28 then.

"How do you think they do it *these* days?" I ask him. I'm 46 now, my son is 19. The year is 1990. The wheel turns.

Waxings in Early May

for Dr. Hsi Cheng

We are out at dusk clearing the last of the winter debris from the back yard, watching for the goldfinch we'd seen at the feeder, when a discreet flock of cedar waxwings settles on the neighbor's apple tree among festoons of white, pink and fuchsia. Through the binoculars, we see that they are plucking stamens from the blossoms, sometimes gobbling petal after petal. Now and then one strops its beak clean of ambrosia. And drifts off as if in reverie. Sometimes as few as three of them, as many as ten. This is nothing like their fall behavior when they migrate south – dipping communally in our birdbath, scouring the juniper of fermented berries, crashing into bedroom windows. The sun is about to set and the clear light shooting horizontally across the robin's egg sky hits them so the tawny colors of their breasts are much yellower than their earthen fall plumage, each bird outlined by a thin golden aura. One preens its breast feathers displaying the black undercoat. Another rudders on a branch showing the bright yellow band on its tail. Impeccable dressers, with identical Chinese-red slashes on their wingtips. If I had been an aging master during the Sung dynasty, I would have thrown away all my other paintings and kept this as my single masterpiece.

Wyo Ming Dynasty – Or –
Why Are No People In Wyarno?

Anna, James and I are tooling around the backroads of the Clear Crik Valley looking for bars, for UFOs, naming criks like Quintuple Crik, Sextuple Crik, Penultimate Crik. Flocks of turkeys everywhere, herds of antelope and deer this few days before the season opens.

It is almost sunset. We pass the M-Bar-M Ranch and see the dark shapes of the buffalo they raise. Anna mentions the undecipherable emblem made of chain hanging from the gate to the McKettle place. Just then the word *barbecue* pops into my mouth. It is instantly clear to the three of us that this style of cooking had its origin on a Bar-B-Q Ranch somewhere near here early in this century.

As you might expect (I discover later), it turns out otherwise: from the Spanish *barbacoa*, derived from the Haitian *barbacoa* – "a framework of sticks" – originally "a framework to hold meat over a fire to be smoked, dried or broiled" – another meaning: "a smooth floor, exposed to the sun for the drying of coffee beans" – and so it goes – at least we invented baseball and the hula hoop – we think.

*

We pass Joe's Place, in Leiter – population minus 10 – the silhouettes of several hunched-over shapes in big hats at the bar, backs to the picture window – the real thing. "Never trust a town where the population's higher than the elevation."

Down in Gilette, Anna tells us, during the boom days of the '80s, the male to female ratio was 15:1. Barmaids made excellent tips but had to be escorted home by armed guard after closing time.

The bars were packed and the testosterone flowed – the fights got worse and worse 'til they brought in the Red Adair of bar fights to figure it out – paid him big bucks to do this. He saw that the brims of those big hats in close proximity on barstools, on dance floors, everywhere, were the problem: brim kept bumping brim. His solution: a hatcheck counter near the entrance of every bar. There were no more fights.

These days the ratio is somewhat better and both the boom and hormone level have tapered off.

Port Salut

You would not marry, monogamize or bear another child, you said – the evening air was bitter, sweet, that I inhaled from you. But maybe I will reconsider the question to this answer of why these beasts are waking. Within a week and we are lost in cosmic traffic. Everything eats the planet, you said. Shades of Johnny Antonelli, Alfredo Antonini. I leaned in toward the blue silk seacoast of your breasts. There were roses on your face, a dwarf mosquito on your brow, your hair pulled back in a cinnamon bun.

> *Ask and it shall be given.*
> *Make the sun, the moon, the night air share.*
> *And should we could we dare we dare?*

Wardwell

in loving memory of Robert E. McCullough, Timothy P. McCullough, Mary Louise and William Prince Hamilton and Grace and T. Wade Clegg Jr.

Mississippi, a likely place for ships from Jupiter to land. Defoliated kudzu makes the land look spooky, useless, as if it wanders and goes nowhere, yet, on the way here, there was purple smoke above the cotton fields. A green swamp this late, where you'd hope that sheep were grazing. The weeds are blood-tinged, the pinestraw, the fallen leaves. A gypsy malcontent, I wander through a winter sunset to your grave. A faint outline, the highlights indistinguishable from false starts scratched in the smoky foreground.

I pass through every ten years or so, like a barnstorming Yankee general. I have no rights to this land, and my heart is not buried here. I see Majic Marts and McDonalds and Gibsons springing up like fungi, and the hardscrabble gospel replaced by swank top 40 palaver. This fight is not mine, this sorrow is not mine, this chained ladder in the cold. I hear the stories and they make my marrow tingle, yet they do not wrench me, crush me to their breasts.

We pull into Tupelo, along McCullough Boulevard, and wind our way to the spot where Elvis lived – now a chapel and a museum behind the two-room shotgun. We are early, as are several others of the faithful. After paying our respects, we drive cross-town to family.

My uncle, with his tall hunched over grin, hugs me but has no idea who I am.

Grace says, "It's Kenneth, Robert's boy."

He says "Oh! He must be a hard worker, then!"

That's the way they knew you, the way I knew you – putting the freezer on your back and walking it by yourself down the narrow basement stairs. And you would take the bat and whack the ball, straight-armed, over the treetops. But if there'd been a way for you to sing a song I'd remember, in your voice. As it was, I remember your Gather-at-the-River bass that made us roll our eyes at each other in the back seat when we traveled. I do not carry a single song or story in your voice, and what flows from you to me is patchwork, fieldwork, hearsay, guesswork, quirks.

*

Turn south at the light on the highway in Vardaman, "Sweet Potato Capital," make a visit to the cemetery at Midway Baptist Church. Your gravestone, military issue,

ROBERT E. MCCULLOUGH
1908–1972
M. SGT. U.S.A.F. RET.
WWII, KOREA, VIETNAM

– no room for Mom's name… but that's another issue. Minnie Ann informs me that my mother had called the two local undertakers to check out prices. Only in Mississippi would we be having this conversation, have traveled here. Your stone, the first in this plot – and now my aunt, my uncle, my cousin (who died of AIDS, which no one round these parts discusses much). A lonely go for Minnie Ann, his mother. But he, Tommy, my cousin, went out with grace (small "g"). The worry lines in Grace's forehead are there in Judy's. There is good company here, and more to come. They tell me where they think my spot should be.

Reading gravestones outside our plot, I notice that family feuds continue down the generations. I remark on the different spellings of *our* family's name (McCullough, McCollough, McCulough, McCullogh) – guess we were either eccentric or illiterate (or both) and seek out the marker of Rufus, the older brother you'd never mentioned, who lived for just a week.

*

Then we visit the site of our family homestead – no souvenirs, no scrap of evidence that we were ever here. Nothing now but weeds, red clay, and sand – not even a stump where the big oak used to stand. A field devoid of treasures. Minnie Ann, my cousin, says, "Mind, the well was somewhere over there…" I walk that way on purpose to fall in where nothing but the cold November air ignores me. For me, the traveler, a final scouring of memories.

I crouch in the weeds and sight along the trees, place my chin on the front parlor windowsill looking back…

the light from the other end of that room; a buggy clomping by on the dry red road to the east; a cow's face at my window waking me after a storm, and me shrieking; a pigpen and an outhouse, contiguous… I remember the sound of my first whippoorwill in the green dusk when I was two, 48 years ago, or was it my first bobwhite one limpid morning when I was three, 47 years ago, or was it the other way around?

I remember my bull Bilbo in the oak the morning after a tornado and can recall Miss Ann's sunbonnet and the taste of water from a dipper, hummingbirds in the four-o'clocks, the salvia, the amaryllis, a sit-down meal on the porch with citronella burning in a bowl and sweet milk I had squeezed myself from long rubbery teats, butter beans, greens, black-eyed peas and you sitting

there talking flexing the mound of the milking muscle in your
right hand, Uncle Clifton's hair buzzed short with his bald spot in
back looking like worn velour, and Prince Junior's grape juice
mustache.

There were celestial hosts around the house — of angel lilies,
angel trumpets, apostle lilies and the Christmas cactus. There
were hyacinths, and snowballs nutmegged by the fall and water-
melon-pink crape myrtle. The one-eyed barncat coughed up a
hairball prompting an anonymous cacophony in the catalpa tree.

Up the road, I'd overhear the neighbor's mynah bird say
"Graaaaaam-mawwwww" with a heavy delta accent. Mr. James,
who lived back in the woods, was black but had green eyes and a
white man's walk. The night-blooming cereus and the century
plant were beyond me, and St. Elmo's fire, St. Vitus' dance and
St. John's bread were forms of idol worship since we were Bap-
tists, intractable, did not believe in saints and beat the sword ferns
into plowshares.

"Wardwell, where the Wards and Wells joined up"

mockingbird   turtle   honeysuckle

After that, to Oxford where you took courses. 'Twas back
before Bill Faulkner'd won the Nobel and was still thought
of by the swells as derelict — he shoveled coal at the Ole Miss
power plant. On his constitutional he'd stop at our tiny house
to talk with you about your chickens and your peanuts. Tad-
pole Smith was AD at the U and Connerly was quarterback.

Red berries trellis through the sycamores... "Mind, the
well was somewhere over there." I strip the tendrils with their
berries and pass most of them to my other cousin Judy, who
knows this place, was here to take away some pieces when
the final owners leveled it. In the photographs, the slant of

the hillside and the stylish hats tell me nothing. If you were here now with us, you'd be two weeks shy of 85, and you could show me where you used to hunt and what you thought about and who lived back in there, now swallowed up by kudzu. The old black faces: the voices you paid respect to when you were home on leave. You traveled, I travel. This life can't completely unravel if we stay in one spot. But this way became a tangle, like the early signs of kudzu.

We stand here and Minnie Ann asks me if I'd read what cousin Wade wrote about this place, where he spent the first few years of his life while Big Wade was in North Africa. A whole generation – no fathers to run to for those first few years of life, to hug us back. Don't you wonder what it did to all of us? Minnie Ann (or is it Anne?) hands me a folded piece of paper with verse neatly lined across the page, and it is what Little Wade felt on his pilgrimage here a year or two ago. She is starting to look like her mother, my Aunt Mary Louise, in fact, at least once a week, my uncle will say to her, "Didn't we used to have a daughter?" – and Wade and I are starting to look alike, though I'll wind up at fullback and he at running back. His family is grown, my son is grown, but I want another family, I guess, to fill in these gaps, these holes, lacunae, where the text was washed away or mildewed out of legibility. Someone could make it up, but I cannot, or won't, or am afraid to.

Wade lives up below Seattle now, and grows exotic spuds for the downtown restaurants and loves the work. If you had made it to retirement, that would have been the life for you, too.

> Minnie Ann is looking like her mother
> and I, like you, my cousin-brother;
> But you've a beard, and I, a ponytail…
> if I could know these lives, as if by Braille.

And the start of my new family here to share this – Greg, from Louisiana, knows what all this means, and her son knows what she knows automatically.

As it starts to rain, I read Wade's words in the best voice I can muster: "Hallowed ground now consumed by nature's zealous growth…"

Minnie Ann and Grace stand behind me and I can hear them sniffling as I fight the peach pit in my throat. I admire his words, and long to be inside them, these memories, the way they are for him, for Grace, for Minnie Ann and even Judy.

I could come here at some other time of year and sit and wait for something, but I have so little to go on – stories of you hunting up the meat for the family, whether it be crow, or blackbirds baked in a pie, lean muskrat, or possum in its gravy. When it comes up from my gullet, it's the sweet taste of muscadine. I never sat in the Midway pews or heard the preacher call me to be saved. Elsewhere, everywhere else, yes, but not here. My roots never had the chance to set here, nor larger ones to choke me off before I blossomed.

I can't conjure the circle of daffodils, the buttercups, the red verbena, the swing, the latticework, the pungence of the livestock, the smoke upcurling from the chimney. I can manage the conversations, match the voices with the faces then, the low laughter. Its almost as if I'm an eavesdropper, a voyeur looking through a smudged-up kitchen window. "Mama would wash down the house as if the water flowed out of a tap, and I had to haul it all from over there."

To come out here today, on this somber errand, we had to leave my uncle in the care of a kindly neighbor kid, who comes in and watches TV with him.

I remember that one morning in early September when that other kid came into the filling station and told my cousin Steve that his other grandma, Miss Minnie, had been "stobbed," and

Steve drove out there to find her in her two-room house aswim with blood where the boy had stabbed her five times then raped her. The boy had mowed her lawn before that, but came by and told her he had to raise his price. She told him she'd have to go without – she lived on Social Security and could not afford it. He went home, got drunk, and came back later. He's in Parchmen now, and due out in a couple of years. He is black, Miss Minnie was white. My uncle's brother is a guard at Parchmen. From then on Minnie Ann always carried a pistol beside her on the front seat on her way from work. Uncle Prince, sweet soul, went on as best he could. Steve's life, since then, has been a wheel of torment. These weights, these curses, carried down the rivers of our blood, even as our souls begin to close.

*

"Walter Wells, an uncle, a u.s. Marshall, came up to two men in a vacant lot beside the Pounds Hotel; they were gambling, shooting craps – a white man and a black man. The black man, Volley Lyons, had his shotgun nearby and went for it – blasted Walter in the face. They carried Walter to the Masonic Lodge where he lasted five, or was it seven, days before he died. Both Volley's wife and Walter's were expecting. They hanged Volley in the town square and T.P., Mama and your daddy had to be there.

Four months later, on the exact same day, both wives gave birth to girls. They named Walter's daughter Walter Lou, after him – not sure about Volley's. You know Zelma, over in Jackson, the judge? She's Walter Lou's older sister. Volley's kin are still around here."

1993–1996

Parallax

A friend suggests we hunt morels in the woods, but I'd rather not. It is mid-May and I have noticed neither the lilacs in bloom nor the five deer sitting in our back yard, one ready to deliver any minute. During this last year I have aged, but not well – the only thing I've tended is your fig tree, misting mites from off the leaves and brushing away their delicate tents. Though you don't want me, other women do, but I could care less. When I read, the words waver as if heat is rising from them. I can't sleep, and my feet have turned to claws. Our infant son has asthma, now, from the dusty carpet. Or could it be the duplicity he breathes?

Suspended Sentence

for Galway, Orion, and Jesse

> And Jesus was a sailor
> when he walked upon the water…
> and when he knew for certain
> only drowning men could see him
> he said All men will be sailors
> until the sea shall free them…
> "Suzanne,"
> – LEONARD COHEN

It was June, and the Root River, which you could usually walk across, was swollen by weeks of rain. I was in a solo canoe, and my son, the Eagle Scout, and stepson (Tenderfoot) were in another. In rapids, my canoe flipped like a plastic bathtub toy. I went down in roiled water and saw my gear, half afloat, about me. I surged to the surface, tried to grip the gunnel – too slick, no purchase. A breath, and down again.

When I surfaced, I heard my son yell, "Are you OK ?"

"No!" I blurted as I clawed at rounded fiberglass. Down again. For the third time, with rank water in my mouth.

What level of Purgatory might await me? Will I come back as a Pekinese, or a toadstool or a mayfly? If I give up, what will I be giving up? My life?

My son will drag my sodden carcass from the river, use his training to bring me back. But the panic… if, in breathing and pounding life back into me, he fails – what then? That memory will anchor him to Hell for all his days. My stepson has already lost two fathers – what will his understanding of fate become? And my sweet baby, just three, his father ripped untimely from him.

As I struggled up again I remembered the thwart, and grasped it, and kicked my way to shallows. My breathing was shallow: my asthma had kicked in. I found my soggy knapsack, opened it, and hurled a roll of sodden toilet paper into nearby branches, raging at myself.

I do not swim, cannot even float – my specific gravity such that I sink slowly and settle on the bottom. When I tell this to my friends they scoff and say, "anyone can float," so we travel to the river and commence this parody of baptism. Yet I never wear a life preserver, and a seat belt only under duress.

I was born on an island, have lived much of my life surrounded by water.

When I was in 4th grade, in Newfoundland, we considered renting a house near Topsail, on the beach, owned by a man named Kenneth Drowns. My mother said she'd have no part of it.

At that time, most of the men in Newfoundland could not swim. Men who spent their lives in dories, in the fog, in squalls on the North Atlantic, fishing for cod. At school, we'd just seen George Cukor's 1935 black and white version of "David Copperfield" – in the movie, David frequents a dwelling on the sea at Yarmouth, from which we witness two horrific drownings and are told that there have been myriad others. The Topsail house was a dead ringer, in my imagination anyway, for the Yarmouth house. I understood my mother's trepidation, but something in me wanted to live there.

As a boy, in Newfoundland, I liked to test thin ice, and often fell into boggy slime to my waist, or worse. Once, a friend and I walked across the St. John's Harbor, and the ice pinged and boomed, making me jump like a bad cartoon.

Shelley, at 29, the most meteoric poet of his day, always tempted fate. He too, could neither swim a stroke nor float. He liked to submerge and hold his breath until a friend dove in to rescue him. Sailing was his passion. He wound up washed ashore near Via Reggio, eaten by crabs and fish, his remains burned on a pyre, but his heart, somehow, still intact in smoldering ashes. I have a photo of myself reclining on his grave, Protestant Cemetery, Rome, holding a cat, pyramid in the background – poetic. I didn't know what I knew.

My friends were unwitting accomplices, also. The day I turned 21, after drinking beer all day, I chugged a quart of Gallo red on a dare, then sinking into blackness, I punched out a Jeep windshield and friends held me back until I passed out. They tossed me in a canal to cool me off, revive me, and, in yellow button-down and white ducks I sank to muddy silt where I rested like a catfish. When my plight registered, one of my chums dove in and rescued me. I came to, hours later, with no recollection of this dousing.

*

I have fallen from high places, been suspended in *that* medium, too. I have walked for half a day through parched air at 13,000 feet without water, and would have drunk my own blood, had it come to that. Wind has scoured me, and my body, wracked by hypothermia, has come back. Fire has surrounded me, then passed by. I have been swallowed by the earth, then disgorged, like a fast-forward Jonah. But until now, water has been my element.

Under the sign of the crab, I was pulled feet first, by five doctors, into this world, from the comfort of amniotic waters – "The hardest birth I've ever attended," one doctor told my mother later. My unwillingness, my denial, started then.

What happens when your lungs fill with water? Those who have survived it and remember say that you become ecstatic, that it is lovely to be at peace; home in the sea within. One friend told me that he drowned at 14. In a tidal pool, on the coast of Wales, he saw himself from a distance, and the light spilling through the water was beautiful and he wondered at having lived so short a life. Nearby, a roly-poly postman crossed the bridge, heard shouts on shore and hauled my friend out. It was 6 PM He came to at 5 the next morning.

Or maybe the human brain, deprived of oxygen fulfills its fantasies, turns manatees to mermaids.

*

Yesterday I experienced my body as a rusty tanker at anchor in the bay, leaking and in need of repairs. My inner voice said, "My friend, unless you do something soon, you will be gone in five years."

Today, I take this stand – to you, my old son, my young son, and my stepson, to make myself seaworthy. To learn to swim, and then to swim. And to the rest of you that I will be here beside you. No longer will I hold my breath and flounder on the bottom. How many of you have almost drowned before?

I will be watching, and if I see that look in your eyes just before you slip below the surface, I will swim out to you, and carry you to the shore.

Irish Snaps

OUTDOOR CONCERT, ST. LAWRENCE HOTEL, HOWTH

Flanked by his red-eyed leftenants, all afternoon in plummy tones, a rosy curmudgeon has toasted everyone and everything under the sun.

After a pre-pubescent Ricky Nelson, also known as Paul McCaffrey, growls out "That'll Be the Day," our latter-day Brendan Behan raises his golden pint and mutters meekly: "Ain't he a *doi*-mun'"

ON THE SUNDAY TRAIN FROM HOWTH BACK TO DUBLIN

As I chat you up in my ersatz Belfast accent you point at the sign SEATS ARE NOT FOR FEET. I raise my eyebrows, swing down my brogans and begin to pick the scab on my shin.

A lad across the aisle says to his granddad, "I take it he is English."

SATURDAY, AT THE PUB HALF OF THE NANCY HANDS

off Infirmary Road, two altar boys come in after 5 o'clock mass. The waiter slips black ties around the necks of their white shirts and they follow him about like goslings, even into the Gents. A middle-aged patron chuckles: "Best watch it — they might start callin' this place Poofter's Paradise!"

Crogh Patrick was St. Patrick's power spot. On this mountain, he reportedly fasted 40 days and 40 nights and it was from here that he drove all the snakes in Ireland into the sea. The faithful make pilgrimages to the top, up an arduous winding trail lined with sharp rocks. Roddy Doyle, noted humorist, tells about climbing Crogh Patrick and falling in behind an old gentleman who was apparently wearing a beat-up pair of purple house slippers. Upon gaining on the old man, Doyle noted that they were not slippers, but the old man's bruised and swollen feet; it is considered pious to make the trek in one's bare feet.

We stop for tea at a shop in the town before making our ascent. I ask the cashier if there is a place to park for Crogh Patrick. He is shocked and maybe even scared by my question. He has sized us up as Americans and thinks that what I'm asking is whether it is possible to *drive* to the *top* of Crogh Patrick and park up there, take a look see, then blast off, in typical American "been-there, done-that" fashion. Reading this in his eyes, I clarify my question and he directs us, with obvious relief, to the car park at the foot of Crogh Patrick, which is brimming. We queue up with the faithful.

AT THE EDGE OF THE BURREN

We'd made arrangements to stay at a friend's cousin's B&B in Ballyvaughan and I'd called ahead twice to let her know we'd be later than expected. I can judge a person by his or her voice, and I tell Lynn that our host is in her late 30s, a tall woman with long black hair, kind of sultry, with a bit of an attitude, somewhat like Angelica Huston. We arrive at 8:30 and are greeted by a banty of a woman about 4′10″, with curly gray hair and beaming smile.

We have walked slowly about the trivallate cashel in the rain, almost worshipping the courses of stone. The fortification overlooks a beautiful valley and reminds me of Mesa Verde, except for the intense green-ness. I suspect that if the residents of both could have visited each other they'd have been right at home. As we approach our car, a couple comes down a lane from a house behind a nearby hedge. We start to pull out then I say, "Let's offer them a ride." When they get close I roll down the window and make the offer. The woman is pretty and vivacious, the man tall and angular, with a prominent chin and intense eyes. They chuckle and say they are just going to Cassidy's Pub up the road in Carron, but why not. We move things in the back seat for them.

The woman spots our copy of *The Book of the Burren* on the back seat, and says, "Gene, you're in that book." He says he is, almost embarrassed. We find his picture on page 190 – in his workshop in Fanore, where he makes traditional pipes. His name is Eugene Lambe. He tells her that Cassidy's has been operating since 1830, and that out behind it is the largest turlough (disappearing lake) in Europe. In winter, it covers 200 acres and is 5 meters deep, in summer, just a patch of brown grass. It can fill or disappear in three days.

"Only in The Burren," he says. I ask him to sign his picture and he writes, "Thanks for the ride! Eugene, Martina," and that he now lives in Kinnara.

A week later, in Dublin, we are talking to Frank Harte, famous musicologist and singer of ballads, and I mention

Eugene Lambe. Frank breaks into a big smile and exclaims, "Gene Lambe... he's the finest maker of pipes this country has ever seen!"

THERE'S AN OLD SCOTSMAN

blown off course, who hovers in the updrafts along the Cliffs of Moher – he'll swoop up from below and startle you face to face – beware! Never try to touch him – if you do he'll vomit clots of half-digested haggis in your hair.

CONVERSATION OVERHEARD AT GRIANAN AILIGH (prehistoric stone fort west of Derry)

> DOOBLE DA WALL GUARD!
> SEAL DA *GYATE*!
> WE'RE OONDER ATTACK BOI *RA*BBLES!
> *FOIRE* DA CANNONS!

Later, a ten-year old knight leads a seven-year-old *rabble* to the dungeon:
"YOU'RE *NOT* GOING TO BE TREATED LIKE A DAINTY!"

IN DERRY

when you ask questions, they can tell the color of your heart.

At 9 PM, walking the jigsaw streets off Falls Road, Belfast. No one confronts me, or looks me in the eye – everyone's shoulders sag with the weight. I hear wind through barbed wire, or is it the Hound of Culainn mourning our losses?

SCARS

We talk to a woman in her 40s named Ann McCullough, married to Seamus McCullough, drummer for the Irish Wolfhounds. She has met us at a tearoom in a Protestant area, and it is clear that she is nervous and that they know she doesn't belong. She tells us that Seamus would have come, but that he has been quite depressed and doesn't feel like leaving the house. She has a small child with her and explains that she loves children and that this ruddy tyke is a foster child. She grew up a few blocks from Falls Road. Once she had been on a bus that had passed through the Protestant neighborhood on the other side of Falls Road and had seen a beautiful park. One day she played hooky from school and went to the park, which was deserted. There were small rowboats tied up at a pier. She climbed into one and undid the mooring and drifted about, lying on her back, looking up at the clouds. She was 8 years old. The pond was shallow. All of a sudden a Protestant girl waded out into the pond, called her a "Cath'lic pig," and dragged her from the boat. The girl then bit Ann hard on the stomach as they thrashed about in the water. Ann raised the corner of her blouse and showed us the teethmarks on her midriff.

Coming down the coast road in our rental car, I am still bab-
bling away in my Belfast accent, but now it's almost convincing, to me at any rate. As we round a bend, a policeman holds
up his hand for us to halt. He is backed by five British para-
troopers with sub-machine guns, all trained on me. He asks
us what we are doing and where we are from. Despite my
usual penchant for being a wise-guy, which might have led
me to say we were "visitin' our fren' Gerry Adams," I glanced
at the eyes of the first paratrooper and knew that if I *were* up
to something, I might be able to distract him for a split second. Then I took in the others' eyes and knew that they would
cover him instantaneously. In my best Midwestern accent, I
told the policeman that we were Americans on vacation. He
was courteous, glanced at our passports, and waved us on. It
was five days after the bombing, the perpetrators still at large.

WHAT'S IN A NAME?

To be a Republican here means something different —
altogether.

Blue Lammen

Intricate roots, intimate shallows, mountains he still remembers down the trail of leaf rot, a reluctant woman bearing rainwater. He longed for fog, up and over the hilt where the shaggy heads careened closer to him, standing stones against chowder and oatmeal sky. When eagles beak open the sky, high above the place where the river bulges into lake, he drops to one knee and opens his shadow. Bells fading, his double is terrible space. Inundation for seven days before him, immaculate, swollen, woven with sweetgrass.

Snow floats across the skeletons of popples, mixed with the first draft of spring. Joining the deer, magenta into catlinite, he soars home. Prosperity never felled his ancestors, but they left their hoods in spavined hotel rooms and dealt illicit hands to their customers, old gray mares stranded on banks of torpid creeks. Never speak. Don't speak. Raise the ante higher. Messages in cottonwoods before you leave. Back a generation, skin fastened to wings, and somehow they drank from celestial fountains before if fell to him: the chirr of locusts.

The *idée fixe* is stroked on ivory Canson then woodcut. He decides he must shave his head. The reds cross at glib and return to questions: less beauty, more attrition, stingy wind drag. Milligrams shy of inviting her to lunch he substitutes responsibility for half an hour; his head becomes an album of indecorum. She was the key witness to his loss, forcing him into tired hands. His shadows and pitch reflect a gold mantle laid in on linen, for breakneck removal. She had spunk. He had protection. Neither gained.

It made no sense, surviving from by-products. The first one, feral as a latin dance step was easy on the eyes, free-floating base notes. By the pecan tree, a grown man groans and swallows the contrapuntal tide: myth declassified – the scent of concupiscence at his elbow. Step by step, marked by hazel ceremonies he came eye to eye and mouth to open mouth, and the hesitated land rose to meet him. He closed the gate on his mother's blue smokerings waiting, like fate, at the excuse-me window. Waking open in a circle of bleached bone.

Beside the stricken ponds and lacquered berries his beard became a blanket for lost causes. A braille tattoo emerged where the wet blessings staircased up his spine. Most often a bridesmaid with a tongue for epiphanies, until blue archangels swam beneath his fingernails instead of clouds. He went to smaller brushes and crushed amethyst. Everything life-sized as he approached what he mistook as mercy. His fall was wings and beaks again, traps upon tightropes, Pacific breeze in rear view mirror. Beads of mercury oozing from every pore.

Tobacco In The Wings

Even now, when the morning is peeling off its rubber mask, the question remains the same – who is listening? Certainly not the wren, past all hope, trying to sing the sun back down. I watch the wren as it flips behind the embankment.

Today, though, no sign of bees and every utterance is hapless. It's fine with me if you stay out there reading the smoking entrails of words, and you can transcribe Sonny and Brownie into Balinese steeplechase tunes, but what do you want from *me* – a shoeshine or a fuck on the snooker table?

The sky is milk, and clotted pieces of it fall on us as we walk. You bring up the first time we met at the all-nite diner adjacent the bus station, you with exhaust still fuming in your hair. In deference to the mailman you wore the bit and bridle from his Sunday rig and the odor of Knox gelatin revealed itself on your breath. Today you are so strung you erupt at any laying on of hands and you leave a trail as we move together.

Around every bend I expect to see a huge wooden yam with a platoon of Wharton School graduates inside, waiting to drop and disseminate, thereby "cleansing the ethnos." Oh, smear the gesso with pesto and let us eat the art. Eating, ho ho, each other.

A thrush pops up in place of the wren and sings subjunctive I do not comprehend: "If I were in care of, care of, care of care." When we reach the road apples we veer left, follow the north fork at flood stage. A young eagle learns to fly from a cliff. Montgomery Clift rides along the far bank looking for his expression snagged in the coarse beards of barbarians. You pass me the third bottle of muscatel and I yell, "Tomorrow, mañana, Manhattan, Kansas!" Down there, we'll shoot an arrow straight at passing Franciscans who'll dust pollen from their robes. Improbable as it may seem, the only city will be nesting in your wig. And what, anyway, was that icky contusion, that faint tremor of pudding, that pottering by which I itched?

Glimpse

It's mid-spring; the valleys are chartreuse and still saturated with run-off from the snowmelt. There's a festival in progress, under big, open-sided tents. Brown men, some born that way, others from a life outdoors, are smiling and laughing. The women less leathered. Many people trading things they've made.

There's an old mission village along the ridgeline to the left, a small dusty place. I notice a white banner with black lettering that says WELCOME TO THE MARRIAGE OF BLAKE AND SAN MIRABEL. I trudge up the road, which takes longer than it looks; almost 30 years since I've been through here and my legs and wind aren't what they used to be. I enter a small morada where there appears to be a ceremony going on. There are about forty people in the whitewashed adobe room. An elder is talking in the old language, and people are amused by what he is saying. He says, in English, "I'd like to welcome any visitors to this ceremony. We are here to join the villages of Blake and San Mirabel in a ceremony of commitment; from now on we will help each other as husband and wife are supposed to."

Someone asks him a question in their language, and most of the people laugh, covering their mouths. Although I don't know this language, I gather that the questioner has asked which town is the bride and which the groom, or something to that effect but maybe more salacious. The elder turns to a young white man sitting near the door, maybe in his mid-20s, who has been looking off into space. The elder says, "Washee, you been here all your life and your family's been hanging around for several lifetimes. I imagine you have some thoughts on this issue." The young man looks up, caught at his day-dreaming, and everyone has another good laugh. He smiles broadly, pleased to be included.

Hilltown

My son and I wake up in a dormitory in a hotel for transients. This used to be a prosperous mining town; it is clean and plain, well maintained though aging. A lot of recent sky-blue trim. The air smells good.

We are on the street, considering our next move when a car pulls up and seven people get out. All of them are dressed up. Two of the men wear brown suits, have oiled hair and gold accessories; it's a group of gypsies. They move in close to us and I press my back to the building so that no one can investigate any of the pockets of my backpack.

They invite us to a gathering at a large camp above the town. The women take my son and treat him as one of their own; he goes off with kids his own age. As it darkens, the men come up front and begin dancing to the drums, one at a time. I stand in the background, take off my clothes and wait my turn. I will dance as long as I can keep a big erection. I step forward and begin grinding my hips, swinging my erection in the opposite direction; the women take up a high-pitched ululation.

As I end my dance, a storm moves in and there's a tremendous downpour. We make our goodbyes and one of the men drives us back to town. Just as we emerge from the car a flash flood rushes down the hill. My son and I body surf one of the surges down an alley, across a main street, and down another alley, where the four-foot wave spends itself.

That was that day.

Altercation

Once, at the beach, in an alley behind a low-rent bar they had us boxed in – five of them and three of us. Don't remember what it was about, but my big mouth may have started it. They had B.O. Tinney down on the ground kicking at his face. I got thrown clear, felt around in the darkness and came up with a 2 by 4. The biggest one had his back to me so I pasted him as squarely as I could in the back of his head and he went down. The others took off running. B.O. was bloody. Lou looked like Bobby Orr after a bad night.

The big guy was down on the ground crying. I grabbed him by the hair. Blood was seeping out his ears and out his eyes. He kept saying, "I can't see! Oh, shit! I can't see!" We grabbed him by his arms and hauled him out to the street – he was bawling like a goddamn baby. Tinny kicked him once and we hightailed it to the car and lit for home, two quarts of dogpiss apiece for the road.

Don't ask me when, or the name of the town, or even which coast. But he'll be back and I won't see him coming, either.

Familiar

High dunes along the beach – a wall for the life within. Early morning I walk the crest until I come to a high point, look down and see a wolf, head-down lope in my direction – no time to slide off the trail – a big one, shoulder ripple, black and silver light of fur.

I crouch in sand and beachgrass, can hear his tongue-out panting up the trail. I ball my strength and just as his body rises over me I strike out with fists head and shoulders, collide with hurtling ribcage gristle, expelling snarl and grunt – his scent in my nostrils.

You shout out at me from the floor where I have pitched you from the bed unhurt but rudely wakened.

Frankliniana

My distant relative had sex with Ben Franklin not once, but hundreds, maybe thousands of times. They'd known each other as teenagers and had an off-and-on thing for most of their lives. Her diary says that he always looked that way but "in a certain light," after they'd smoked a bowl or two he could be "quite fetching." She includes a sketch of Ben, in rocking chair, in his first set of bifocals.

In bed, he was, as you'd expect, inventive, and had read all the ancient how-to manuals. And if he couldn't get into a position, would rig up a harness or pulley that would accommodate. He wasn't above bondage either, preferring silk and satin sashes, the feel of exotic fabrics. Ben was sometimes lethargic and stayed in bed using his flexible urinary catheter, which snaked across the bedroom – she found this, she says, offensive. There were times, she said, she felt like a trained seal – he had an odometer attached to the bed and kept records, especially of simultaneous orgasms.

Neither he nor they, however, *included* animals, and only once a *ménage à cinq*, when three of her female friends and she captured Ben and they applied their charms, experimenting with ice and different spices. In the oral realm, Ben liked to hum and sing the scales while so engaged, sometimes employing his glass harmonica.

You may wonder why she never got pregnant. Ben didn't fire blanks, but he'd give her rinses and washes he'd worked up from roots and leaves he'd studied. And he'd don, with great flourishes, sleeves of various transparent substances.

Even, once, to a drumroll from an out-of-work Minute Man. Although Ben himself was not a minuteman, but an hour man, or an all-night-rooster-crowing-thrice-in-the-morning man, then he'd hop up to stoke his Franklin stove. Once, on her birthday, the glee club from Ben's volunteer fire department serenaded them throughout the night.

The diary says Ben's member was larger than the norm and swerved to starboard, with a birthmark shaped like the state of Pennsylvania. His stones were goodly and the left one hung down farther as the years progressed.

Eventually, she followed him to Paris, they had a falling out – his games with electricity were just not up her alley – batteries, discharge, negative, positive…it ends in mid-sentence.

The Appointed House

I flew in earlier this morning and met with most of the staff, and now my new cohorts, Mutt and Jeff, are showing me around the area. As we come over a hill, I spot a ramshackle house down a winding lane. I ask them to pull in and they oblige. We get out and I hear a whippoorwill in the out-of-focus distance. It has been some years since I've heard one – it gives me a good feeling about the place. It is dank in the trees, almost dark, ruinous – like France after The War, I speculate. So here we are, three men exploring a haunted house. I imagine they think they have to humor me, at least at the start.

The house is a big open place with the roof starting to collapse – a combination of a barn, a stable and, oddly enough, a chapel – there are what look like the remnants of a small rose window high up at one end of a wing, with the glass and leading busted out. We enter a huge sooty kitchen with stone and bricks showing through the plaster, and rough open beams hewn by hand. The house has a gothic aspect, tall and narrow. There are many slightly different levels and, in several places, hard-packed dirt floors. The doors and windows are at the ends of the wings, so there's not much light inside. My two companions pretend that they have been here before. Not much conversation – each of us lost in himself. I am afraid to say anything because this is the house that I've always wanted to live in, always. But I know that I will not live in this town long, or any other town, for that matter. She could make the fires dance on these walls. Even though I will send for her tomorrow, she is not the one, either.

We return to the plant briefly, to confirm my appointments for tomorrow, then head down out of the timber into the flats. It is muddy everywhere in sight, and there is a lot of deadfall and slash lying about. Mutt and Jeff pull up to a garage that has a sprawling junkyard behind it. Off to the right is the black cone of a pulp burner surrounded by stacks of poles. There is black smoke coming from the cone and the predictable sickly-sweet odor of sulfur.

Mutt says to me, as he points, "This is the place we like to stop and visit on our way home, now and then." They grin at each other. Outlined against the piss fir at the back of the clearing is a giant white work glove above a warren of squat wooden buildings. I can't quite make them out, but as we turn down the muddy road, I have a pretty good idea where we are going. I've never been before, and I'm thirty-six years old.

We pull up in front of the sprawling two-story structure – bigger than I thought. There is evidence of every kind of architecture imaginable, but mostly frontier gothic – unpainted ark wood, grayed with weathering. The work glove is made of thick canvas stretched over heavy-duty wire mesh and sprayed with something to stiffen it. It must be twenty feet high. I want to tell my companions that I'd rather not be here, but I don't.

There's a reception committee: a woman, the madam, I guess, who is attractive, but kind of mannish, and five other people, all nondescript. Nevertheless, I feel like a sea captain as the natives swim out to greet his ship. But this is the clothed northcountry version.

Inside, there are the rich aromas of game roasting and a mixture of several items being baked. The woman takes my elbow and we go into the dining room. She seats me at the head of the table. There are over twenty people already seated, who nod politely. I can see the kitchen in its entirety, and the three cooks, who smile and make formal bows in unison. I bow back. The wood in the room is very dark – the dining table under the white tablecloth, the wainscoted walls. It seems that everyone here has been expecting us. The woman sits to my right and my associates take places farther down the table. There's a fifty-fifty split of men and women.

Now the food is brought in. The people seated near me ask questions about me and about my wife. These are not perfunctory questions – the people seem to have a genuine interest. But as I respond, I have an odd feeling that all my answers are somehow being recorded and that they will filter back to the woman or women who will "entertain" me later.

The meal is immaculate: one dish is pheasant stewed in coconut milk, covered with a sauce of tiny sliced shrimp, onions, red peppers, some crushed seeds I can't identify and an oil I can't quite place. There's maybe a hint of garam masala. And the best cornbread I've ever had. My personal waiter brings me buttermilk – they certainly did their home-work. We have a salad of incredible leafy things and delicate sautéed root vegetables – local, I presume.

The woman to my left is passing me a tureen of gravy and dumps it in my lap. The thick brown warmth covers the crotch and thighs of my trousers, but I am not burned. The woman is speechless and there is a palpable tension in the room until my waiter brings me a towel and they recognize that I am not upset, merely embarrassed.

We are offered five kinds of wild berry pies and afterwards the head cook (you couldn't really call him a chef) comes out and shakes my hand. I usually don't drink coffee, but this has such a rich and fertile essence that I say yes.

The meal is over and I realize that I haven't really been here – too uptight about where I am and what is going to happen. The madam pushes her chair back – time to disperse.

I haven't looked at the people carefully until now. The men seem older than I, prosperous, easy-going – can't read their professions, aside from those seated near me who identified themselves – an architect, an entrepreneur, a tailor. As to the women, just two of them are matronly, with expensive but tasteful hair they couldn't have had styled locally. All the others have the rounded bodies of Greek statues and fresh clear eyes that you wouldn't expect in this part of the country.

Several say that they hope to see me again, and they obviously mean it. A blonde woman, who is taller than my high school girlfriend, squeezes my arm softly and looks up into my eyes. I smile but can feel the blush spread across my neck and shoulders. The madam excuses us and takes my elbow again. She leads me out into the hall. The halls have the same kind of dark wood, and are softly lit. There is not much activity on this floor.

We go up a wide staircase and she says, "There are some special ladies I'd like you to meet," as she opens a polished oak door for me. I step in and three women rush gaily down the hall in the vague light. The short frenetic blonde brushes her palm against my genitals and recoils.

I say, "It's gravy...someone dumped their food on me."

She says, "Oh!" and we both chuckle as she takes my hand. The other two each have an arm around me and are gently propelling me forward. One has red hair and wears it like Rhonda Fleming, the other is mostly Polynesian with long straight black hair but with the blue eyes of a Siamese cat. This is ridiculous – as if I'm at some kind of sexual fantasy camp. But again, I want to say, "Stop, please. I'd rather not." Again, I don't.

Then I am off in a parlor with the blonde, the other two at the ready. I can see them in the mirrors, whispering behind their hands. As she takes off my tie and unbuttons my shirt I say, "Look, I have to explain this to you – I think you're used to a certain type of man coming here...drunk out of his gourd, banging away at you like a slow jackhammer for an hour and a half before he comes, while you recite the first half of Wuthering Heights in your head. For me, it's a two-way street. First, if there's no chemistry, I can't fake it. And second, bringing *you* pleasure is what I'm after – not getting my rocks off." What am I saying! I sound like a character in a bodice ripper – I'd better shut up.

I notice the lines on the blonde woman's face, particularly the vertical lines along both her lips. She is probably in her 60s but has the upturned breasts of a woman in her 20s or 30s, and soft resilient skin. She eyes me coyly, and says, "Hey, soldier, it's not that way at all. You think of yourself as an artist.... I'm an artist, too – this is my art. What you've just told me – I knew all those things before you got here. Maybe it's that way in big city masquerade parlors, but not here. But you've never been to those places anyway, have you?"

I have stepped into a place I shouldn't be; something is changing which I can't stop. I could still get up, get dressed and politely decline this situation. Her gray eyes look deep into mine and she says, "May I have the next dance?"

Waterborne

Fog had persisted the entire day, muting the colors, muffling the sounds – my kind of day. I was holding down a bench taking a smoke when Vaporetto Number 20 approached. Since we were no great distance from Venice proper, I was surprised by the rate of speed at which the craft traveled then swerved into place at the dock. I was even more surprised when I saw that a trim young woman with auburn hair was piloting the boat. She patted the real pilot on the shoulder as he stood next to her with a cowed expression on his face, then she hopped onto the dock. I was immediately captivated by the confidence of this woman and her carriage as she walked briskly toward the doors of the library.

I had spent the last two weeks coming here to San Lazzaro degli Armeni, the small island near the Lido, occupied by an Armenian monastery and its 150,000 volume library, which includes many ancient texts. I had been working on an extended piece about Lord Byron and was following his trail near the end of his life; he had spent much of his last year at this monastery. The island had been a leper colony from the 12th to the 16th century and was abandoned until an exiled Armenian nobleman was given the property to found a Benedictine order here in 1715.

I followed the woman into the library and observed her from a discrete distance. She was speaking with one of the white-bearded monks, a venerable curmudgeon who had helped me in my research. She was not Italian, I knew that, but she spoke Italian with a perfect Venetian accent. As they conversed, they both slipped on white gloves and began handling archival materials – codices, folios and bound volumes he had laid out in anticipation of her coming. They shared a large illuminated magnifying glass. From what I could gather, he was pointing out the intricacies of binding, inking, and letter forms, and the specifics of damage which time had wrought on these treasures, whether papyrus, vellum or paper. He was clearly entranced by this woman, probably wishing that he were not a monk and thirty years younger.

When the woman left, taking the last vaporetto of the day, I followed. There were only six other passengers. I did my best not to tip her off that I was studying her. When we disembarked, I gave her some lead-time, but Venice is not the kind of place you can follow someone at a distance, and she took prodigious strides for such a petite person. Eventually she entered a rough neighborhood near San Nicolò dei Mendicoli, inhabited mostly by stevedores. She untied an aluminum skiff from a dock, sprang down into it, took out a yellow hat and slicker from a cargo box, fired up the engine and roared off into the evening.

As it happened I too had a small battered skiff, rented from my landlord. Mine was tied up in the Nuovo Ghetto, in front of my friend Fausto's house. I had a place on the west end of Burano in a converted shed where my landlord's father had built boats. They were no longer in the business; the skiff was one the old man had built and was on blocks under tarps in the yard. It took some coaxing to get my landlord to rent it to me, as he considered it an heirloom, but he knew I was on a tight budget and charged me next to nothing.

My "studio" was plain but comfortable and removed from the flow of tourist traffic. It made more sense commuting this way than depending on the ferry. It was pretty much a straight shot across the lagoon to my lazy island. This was my third time in Venice. I've been told that no matter how long you live there, it keeps unfolding. For me, every day had borne witness to this truth.

The next day the sun was out and I was up early working on my notes. In the afternoon I decided to empty my mind by doing watercolors. The pastel colors of the houses on Burano, if one renders them carefully and often enough, can take the work of even the rankest amateur up several notches. This was my therapy; I had hundreds. All the while I was thinking about the woman and the way she moved.

In the morning, even before sunup, I had my cappuccino and headed into Venice. I swung around the west end of the island, entered the Canale della Giudecca, cut up Rio di San Sebastiano, took a left and pulled into the same area where the woman had docked. I asked around until I found someone who directed me to an old man who rented me a spot for the day. San Lazzaro does not allow private launches, so odds were she would dock here again before going there or anywhere else. I bought a paper and stationed myself at a table across the way. Sure enough, an hour later she swooshed into her slip, then went to a hole-in-the-wall café for cappuccino and pastry. The café was frequented by stevedores and ex-stevedores. The manager was a big swarthy fellow who hovered around the woman without distracting her from her morning paper. He stole appreciative glances. At one point she took out her cigarettes and before she could locate her matches, he'd swooped up and given her a light. She was obviously on to him, but, much to her credit, she played the game. She smoked Woodbines and held her cigarette between her index, middle finger and thumb as if it were a hypodermic. And pointed her lips to the right when she exhaled. All of her gestures were slightly eccentric but sexy.

Next, she went to check her mail at the post office. She received a bulky packet which she ripped open immediately, spreading the contents onto the cramped table, oblivious to gawkers and busybodies. I could see that it was a hand-written manuscript, in a large and bold hand, accompanied by some intricate illustrations and what appeared to be three or four detailed topographical maps. After she'd occupied this table for about fifteen minutes, an official came out and asked her politely to relinquish the spot. She seemed startled, embarrassed that she had fallen into this reverie, and apologized. He spoke to her in English and it seemed to me that her response, also in English, had a marked British accent. She gathered the material quickly and strode off through the rain with it under her raincoat. She walked almost as fast as she ran her boat. Her exaggeratedly long strides were comical, yet charming – a remnant, I imagined, of the unselfconscious little girl she had once been – but now she was very much a woman.

I trailed her for the better part of a mile before she turned into a well-known printing establishment. I was surprised that she had not picked up on my presence by now. Or maybe she had. In matters such as these, women love to lead us into thinking that we are a step ahead of them. Anyway, I stationed myself across the street in a miserable pest hole of a pizzeria and watched her through the steamy front window. I could see her gesticulating and arguing with one of the proprietors. This went on for half an hour. Finally, the two of them came to an understanding, shook hands vigorously, then the woman, in her inimitable brusque fashion, strode from the shop and back the way she had come.

Her next stop was the Academy of Fine Arts. A string quartet was practicing. There were about a dozen people scattered throughout the auditorium. She took a seat in the center of the first balcony, and alternated between sitting with her eyes closed, on the verge of sleep, and writing notes furiously. I had no idea what she was writing, as I could not get any closer. I must admit that I was tempted to steal over quietly and kiss her eyelids while she was in one of those raptures. The group was rehearsing a Vivaldi piece. After they had finished, to a smattering of applause, the woman trussed up and made her way back to the quay where she'd docked. She was whistling the Vivaldi in a strange sing-song way, which made it sound like Chinese orchestral music.

It was raining. She slipped on the slicker and hat, started the engine and was off. I was not far behind. She threaded her way out to the canal then gunned it. Despite her self-assurance, I'd thought of her as delicate and vulnerable. But seeing the way she handled that boat through heavy chop, perched in the stern in hat and slicker, gave me a different perspective. We were bouncing along in open water and I was having a hard time keeping up, on the verge of seasickness. No way she would suspect anything in that fog. And then I realized that she was heading for Burano! She made for the leaning campanile, turned down the Fondamenta di Terranova and threaded her way to the front of a house the color of dried blood. I killed my engine and waited. She tied up, stowed her rain gear and entered the front door. I saw a light come on in the front room of the second story. I checked the number: 22. So far, this was too good.

*

I wasn't sure what to do next. Finally, I decided to memorize just one song. I considered "'O Sole Mio" because it was romantic, dramatic, verging on the cornball, and everyone knew it. I didn't figure I'd spread myself thin by working on more than one piece. But I decided that singing a Neopolitan song in the presence of Venetians, who had nothing but scorn for most things southern, was a bad idea, even though the woman was not Venetian and might forgive me. I could have taken something from my Mario Lanza tape, like "Be My Love," but that might be too popular – maybe *I* was getting too particular. Or something from Mozart – *The Marriage of Figaro* or *Don Giovanni*, since the libretti had been written by Lorenzo da Ponte, a Venetian Jew who trained as a priest. He was kicked out of every Italian city for his politics and womanizing, wound up in Vienna and wrote the words to Mozart's four most famous operas in a year's time. He surfaced subsequently in London, New Jersey, Pennsylvania and finally New York City where he was appointed Columbia University's first professor of Italian and founded what was to become the Met. He had been friends with Cassanova and that, coupled with his own predilections, made him the perfect person to write *Don Giovanni*.

But I couldn't find anything that was appropriate or within my range. Listening to a tape of Pavarotti, I hit on "Che gelida manina," from *La Bohème*. I'm no Pavarotti, but can sing that sort of stuff if I work at it. I spent the rest of the week rehearsing over and over, with Luciano's rendition in my head. At first I had to fake my way through the phrase *la dolce speranza*, but used Roy Orbison's *Greatest Hits* as my warm-up tape, which got me close. My practicing gave the landlord and his family no end of amusement.

I made one trip to San Lazzaro during the week but she did not come that day. I stayed away from the cafés on Burano around Piazza Galuppi, figuring that I might see her – I didn't want that. And I did not go near her house.

I then hired musicians, two violins and a flute, and after rehearsing together a few times, we went, on a crisp moonlit Wednesday night, to the woman's place of residence. She was usually home by 9 PM. I had paid a kid to be a spotter and let me know that she was actually there. We tuned up and I began to belt out my offering: "*Che gelida manina/se la lasci riscaldar /Cercar che giova…*" Sure enough, she threw open her shutters as I broke into "*Talor dal mio forziere/ ruban tutti i gioielli…*" She was smiling broadly. Other shutters had opened. When I finished, I was cheered, by consensus, into performing an encore. Since this was my only piece, I sang the last part of it again, this time in English:

> I am a poet. What am I doing?
> Writing! How do I live then?
> Somehow!
> I have no worldly riches:
> Ev'ry poetic measure
> Holds a fabulous treasure.
> In dreams of flights and fantasy
> And castles in the air,
> I am indeed a millionaire!
> And now two eyes have stolen
> Ev'ry priceless possession
> Of my esteemed profession…

And finished with "Won't you tell me who you are? Please say you will!" I was banking on her not taking my choice of characters the wrong way.

There was even more applause. She leaned out the window in a loose-fitting blouse, revealing the shadow between shapely breasts. She called my name softly, and told me to come up. She knew my name! I paid the group so they would serenade us for the next two hours; any less time would have been pessimistic – I didn't want to jinx myself. Thus began our courtship.

*

Our remaining time together in Venice was full. I had enough money for two months, she, for three. We were both loners by nature and had our own work, but spent every moment we could with each other. Some of those moments were, of course, on San Lazzaro degli Armeni. The old monk was visibly jealous.

And we haunted cemeteries, our favorites being the tumble-down Jewish cemetery on La Guidecca, where we found several stones almost 400 years old, and San Michele, where they disinter you after 13 years if you aren't a big shot. We speculated where the bones went – maybe pulverized and spread on the fields, maybe the source of a clandestine scrimshaw industry.

I am a lapsed Reformed Jew, she, a lapsed Mennonite. Both of us had become Franciscans by inclination, fond of expressing our devotion. There were churches where we sank to our knees beside each other – San Eustachio on Canale Grande, under a Tiepolo, and San Zaccaria, where Bellini's "Virgin Mary" graces the altar on the left side. At Fausto's invitation, we accompanied him to temple.

I learned that the object of my own personal adoration was not British but from Hot Springs, South Dakota – and had acquired her British accent via cosmic osmosis. We kept our separate places, but I told my landlord I no longer needed the skiff. I learned that she leased hers from a family she'd known for years. I started smoking her Woodbines, and could do a perfect imitation of her smoking. We eschewed gondolas completely.

We loved our Burano, but hopping to other islands became an avocation. My lady introduced me to Torcello. She explained its rich history, that it had been the mother of Venetian culture. But these days it's a ghost, with less than 100 people living there. Once we splurged and stayed at a lovely hotel, Locanda Cipriani, but the other two times we camped out, to watch the sun set over the marshlands – rose, periwinkle, lavender, apricot. The sound of church bells across the laden distances of the lagoon. The silhouettes of ancient Santa Maria Assunta and Saint Fosca, slightly askew on the horizon.

We also spent an afternoon on nearby San Francesco del Deserto, with its trim collar of cypresses. We went in homage to our patron saint, Francis, who had once waited out a storm there. A good place to lie on or backs and cloud-watch.

We visited many of the islands in our tin skiff, often popping into the churches to sit, pray, or meditate. More often than not I was faking it – kneeling next to her I experienced such a strong buzz that the hairs on my arm stood up from the static electricity. I remember San Michele in Isola and San Giorgio Maggiore in particular.

Venice had become, for me, a separate galaxy, each island a distinct planet, with its own quality of air, of light, of olfactory sensations. If one could only bottle these essences.

In many of these places (even the cemeteries) we made sweet and abandoned love. Sometimes in our skiff. Once, a fisherman surprised us *in flagrante delicto*. We hurried to cover ourselves, but he merely fanned himself with his hand, rolled his eyes and pretended to gasp for breath.

On all of our outings we carried tangerines in our knapsack; hence, the two of us invariably had our own scent – tangerines mixed with a delicate overtone of shellfish, and maybe a dash of ripe figs and fresh violets. Sometimes she brought along an apple, which she'd peel in one perfect spiral with her pocketknife. We loved pears and marosticane, the wonderful cherries of the region. My love for her and my love for Venice had become indivisible. I held my breath, waiting for some figurative grain of sand to cause an irritation between us that would begin the erosion of our relationship, but even our serious arguments seemed to resolve themselves.

When we drifted in the skiff I'd read *Don Juan* to her. I found the text hard to recite for some reason. Not sure why. She listened dutifully but I could tell she was just being polite. I soon tired of it. But I *was* becoming Byronesque – I'd let my hair grow out from the usual quasi-military crew cut and taken to wearing the collarless rough cotton peasant shirt she'd bought me. In restaurants, for effect, I would stare into her depths seductively and broodingly à la Byron. We could sense waiters stopping in their tracks. We had long conversations in Italian, her accent decidedly Venetian, mine more Staten Island.

I was becoming privy to *her* Venice. My lady's restaurant-of-choice was Corte Sconta, in Castello, the east end. Claudio, the big chef with the David Crosby moustache, and his sassy wife Rita considered her family. And they adopted me as if I were a beloved brother. Corte Sconta is where we stopped for *cechiti* and *ombre*. *Cechiti* are the Italian cousins of *tapas*. We shared a love for octopus, cuttlefish, sweet and sour sardines, and braised eel. Claudio usually served cubes of hard goat cheese, *Pecorino* and *Caprino*, and semi-soft *Montasio* along with the *cechiti*.

An *ombra* is a small glass of wine served to accompany the *cechiti*. Rita, always with a flirtatious smile, dispensed the *vini della casa*, *Refosco*, *Soave*, *Prosecco* or *Tocai* (now and then a red, but I can't remember which) from a brass-topped table. An interesting bit of etymology – *ombra* means "shade," or *ombretta* – "little shade" – in the old days when there was a thriving market in the San Marco piazza, merchants would follow the shadow of the campanile as the day progressed, keeping their wine cool in that way. Customers would go "into the shade" for a pick-me-up and some banter.

Now and then we'd step out – twice we treated ourselves to *fegato con salvia e spinaci* (calf's liver with sage and spinach) at Trattoria alla Madonna, near the Ponte Rialto. The real reason I went was that it reminded me of home: the waiters were loud, cranky old men with character, not unlike the Jewish waiters at Katz's Deli on the old Lower East Side.

We seemed to share the same palate: *seppie con polenta* (cuttlefish served in its own ink – a mysterious black dish), *spaghetti alle vongole* (clams), and *baccalà* (salt cod) in any of the many ways Venetians have of preparing it. We preferred our *polenta "come la seta"* – "like silk." But occasionally I'd get a broiled piece that was a bit gritty, reminding me pleasantly of home-made cornbread from childhood visits to my grandparents on my father's side in Mississippi. We also devoured Tintoretto, Titian, Canaletto, Veronese and Carpaccio. *This* diet doesn't sound very Franciscan, I realize, but our usual fare was pretty spartan. I was eating less and less, preferring to feast on her.

We played hard, yes, but this fed our energy to do our own work even harder. And I no longer painted watercolors for therapy.

Rita was always extolling the virtues of her hometown, Chioggia. A week before I left we made a day-trip pilgrimage there by water. It was just as Rita had described it – almost an imaginary place – a miniature, less-touristed, less-polluted Venice. A kind of parallel reality, but one in which we seemed to be able to always get our bearings, as opposed to Venice. Before we returned, we had *baccalà mantecato* at a small restaurant near the famous fish market. We were sitting next to each other in a booth. Her skirt was up around her thighs. I could hear her touching herself with her fingers – she never wore underpants. As she pressed her fingertips to my nostrils, she said *"Sarebbe per me il piu irresistibile dopobarba con il profumo del mercato di Chioggia*" (For me, an after-shave with the smell of the Chioggia fish market would be the ultimate turn-on).

On Burano itself, not far from her house, she introduced me to more of her extended family. Trattoria da Romano had been frequented by Chaplin, Fellini, and Uncle Ezra, and was the best place in all of Venice for *risotto di pesce*. Orazio, the jolly proprietor, lit up like his wood fire whenever he saw my consort. He would enlist her to make *tiramisù*, and exclaimed that it was the best *tiramisù* he'd ever tasted. Several of us speculated that maybe it was the way she whipped the *mascarpone*, or perhaps slipped several drops of some narcotic into the coffee or the brandy. Orazio always brought us *caffè corretto* laced with *grappa* to finish the meal, and one for himself with which he toasted us. This is where we had our last meal together before I left. Orazio presented me with a jar of fruit – grapes, apricots, peaches, figs and raisins – preserved in *grappa* with a little sugar, to take with me on the plane. It was a great send-off. Before my life in Venice I had believed in the value of emptiness, but now I was full.

* * *

Being itinerant scholars with no attachments, we had the opportunity of starting from scratch. We have settled into a hamlet on the West Coast not far from Seattle. I say hamlet because it has a population of only 84 people. It is called Lewiston, after Capt. Meriwether Lewis, who passed just a few miles from here. This, like so many towns and species of flora and fauna in the northwest that take their names from either Lewis or Clark.

The combination of elements in this landscape, some strictly American, some European, many Oriental, have made our choice to live here an easy one. Given so few people, we nonetheless have a good mix of cultures – Anglos, Latinos, Russians, Japanese, Hmong. We rent a sprawling old bungalow in the middle of an orchard (apples, pears, hazel nuts) which gives both of us the experience of being cloistered somewhere in the south of France. The whole town seems hidden. And there's no downtown or even a main street. I've started a small garden: plum tomatoes, arugula, radicchio, fennel, basil, thyme and sage.

Today you are in Seattle, discussing bindings with the owlish eccentric whose memoirs you've deigned to print. Interesting stuff, written in the quirky style of one educated entirely by private tutors. You've become such a part of me that just the one night you've been away has sent me into paroxysms of erotic fantasies, but you will return this afternoon.

Through the jungle at the back of our property is a good-sized pond. I've spent the morning out here fishing. Actually just drifting around in the boat catching up on my reading. No cigarettes: we've both stopped smoking.

The heavy air today and being on the water has reminded me of our time together in Venice. I really love the water, though I spend precious little time on it anymore. I often hear whispered intimations of Shelley's fate. My study of Byron has made these whispers louder. I remember a line from Trelawny: "Like the Indian palms, Shelley never flourished far from water." – That is my story, too. And like Shelley, I am inept in the water – I have never learned to swim very well. As opposed to Byron, who swam the Hellespont. Byron would have mocked me, as he did Trelawny, as he did Dr. Polidori (calling him "Dr. Polly-dolly"). Byron's swagger, his moods, his clubfoot, and his man-of-action feats attract me as much as *Don Juan* and *Childe Harold*. Because I am Dr. Polidori, the pale sidekick.

Thinking of Venice just brought to mind the map I was looking at yesterday: we have our own system of small canals right here at the edge of town, to handle the run-off this time of year from melting snows in the mountains. The water is really up right now.

Our dingy is light enough that I can carry it on my back. I strap in one oar to steer with, and bring along a life preserver. It's a quarter mile to the nearest canal. I lug the boat down the lane and get buzzed by a mockingbird who doesn't know quite what to make of this awkward creature dragging its shell through her territory. And then I am there, out of breath.

It's more of a sluice than a canal, poured concrete. The water is clear, almost turquoise – minerals from snowmelt, I presume. It's not very deep – three or four feet – but the current is fierce. There's a wide towpath alongside, with which the water is almost level. If I were in the dingy on the water I could probably step out directly onto the towpath. Why not try it? When you get back from Seattle, what I'll do is take you on an outing. I'll blindfold you and somehow get you into the boat. The increasing din will keep you in suspense. Ridiculous!

I snap on the preserver and untie the oar. I launch myself and the plunge in the pit of my stomach makes me realize that I won't have to worry about steering – it's out of my hands. I'm on the water maybe a minute when it starts getting choppier. There's some kind of drop-off ahead – not falls, I hope, and before I can do anything I shoot down a 45-degree incline for about twenty yards. The dingy starts to turn and I can't right it. I'm actually flying and when I hit the plume at the bottom am flat on my back, dug in. People have told me that downhill skiing is more exhilarating than good sex – I can't believe that, but I've avoided downhill skiing.

As I plow through the turbulence into the larger channel I

see three other sluices emptying their contents full bore. I buck the confluence and head "down stream." My oar is gone. The banks of the channel are earthen, no towpath. And now an increasing din ahead of me. Not good! I am four feet from either bank with no way of steering. I know the river is somewhere below me and now I know where I'm heading – Clatsop Falls – I love the water, I love the water, but not to be swallowed like this! As I approach the chasm, or whatever it is, my life force starts leaving me and I feel myself rushing away from you forever. Never to see you again. In a fraction of a second I am translucent, transparent, invisible. Between the trees, a cable drooping across the channel. I stand up. Leap for it with everything and catch it and pull myself up and swing myself hand-over-hand the four feet to the bank. And fall exhausted and weep. The salt of life rushing back into me: tangerines, shellfish, crushed violets.

When I am steady enough to walk, I head up a logging road. I am in someone's back yard, shaking all over. The house, barn, and sheds are unpainted, weathered silver. There is a hand-painted sign: Francesco Street – never heard of it. I ask an old Japanese sprite sitting on his porch for directions. He points at another sign: Canal Street. And says something in Japanese and chuckles. What will you think of my carelessness?

The Third Estate

A raw wind of discontent was rising. They'd bilked the villagers, sold them relics, spices from Bruges, fabrics from Damascus, black velvet doublets and round beaver hats. Blue-nailed low country artisans joined with weavers from Ghent to kill the rich folks off, slaughtered all who did not have calloused hands. They shaved crosses on the young mothers' heads and dressed up a pig who ate the Duke's son while aunts plied them with poppycakes and tea. Whores waited beside the charnel houses. Snot caked on the faces of the children. Boys plugged up the assholes of their dead fathers.

Pablo the Cruel, a hog in armor, his jaquette lined with 1200 ratskins, could not have made it riper than it was – circumspection was not his strongest suit. To receive, he first had to give – for him, as difficult as weaving ropes from sand. A school of scarlet leaves scratched after him as he left the Curia in ruins.

The Almoner's Song

Priests with lungs as black as their cassocks chant at the bonecarts clearing the streets. The village men dream of milk-white thighs while an eyeless child leads a wild procession of mothers eating their own intestines. I ride the crest of my grief, delivered, and fall to my knees in the beards of the hayfield.

I sleep and dream the Book of Bethlehem – there are six elements: corn, meat, and water, air, fire and rope; three weapons: bells, nets, and knives; seven sacred animals: stag, bear, heron, eel, bee, fox and harpy. I approach a tame bear, my hand over his left eye – by this he knows me, and we roll about in the cool grass for most of the afternoon.

I wake to find the town's gates closed, so I follow a trough of mud to the border; currant bushes spatter the hillsides, a lark in the barley, the flame of a fox. My luck rides high on the cracked horizon. A leper in blue smoke watches me pass. And I see you, song of the thistle, savior.

Heirloom

for Lynn

My father wasn't much of a drinker – one Pabst Blue Ribbon on the hottest day of the year, after we'd completed some grueling physical task. I'd say he averaged two beers a year. He died in 1973. In his will, he left me a small glazed ceramic wine jar. I never once saw him drink wine. Not having read his will, I did not know of the existence of this wine jar until about two years after his death. I was home for Christmas. My mother took me aside, when everyone else was out of the house, and showed me the jar. It was ochre in color, squat, and had a thick glaze showing no cracks. It had a tightly fitting lid, sealed with a thick coating of wax. She said, simply "Your father wanted you to have this." And then she told me the history of the vessel, as my father had told it to her.

The wine jar had been passed down for many generations in our family – many. The wine in the jar had been collected at the "Marriage of Cana" in Galilee almost 2,000 years ago, by one of the guests who was a devoted follower of Jesus. After the feast, the man had poured the contents of one of the stone jars containing water that Jesus had turned into wine into this small jar and sealed it up as a keepsake. He, of course, had no idea of its significance. After Jesus's crucifixion and the state of confusion among his followers, the man with the jar decided to give it to Joseph of Arimethea, knowing that he would take care of it. Joseph of Arimethea was imprisoned for 42 years, and after his release by the Emperor Vespasian, traveled to Britain to spread the gospel. He brought the jar with him. There is, of course, the legend that he also brought the Holy Grail. But that is another story. One vessel held water which had been turned to wine, the other, water and blood transformed to wine.

As a gesture of his faith in the local converts, he gave them the jar. This was in the present-day town of Glastonbury, Somerset. After some time, centuries actually, the jar made its way up to Scotland, into the hands of Bishop Aidan, at Lindisfarne. Apparently its presence aroused some jealously, and Aidan passed it to one of our relatives, named Lullach, a minor noble in that area, who had become a believer. This was in the 7th century. The family moved up the coast to a place called Navity, on the Black Isle, a peninsula near Inverness, and eventually from the west of Scotland to the east, to the vicinity of Wigtown, around 1300. At some point they crossed into Northern Ireland, and settled in county Antrim. They left Ireland because they were persecuted as Presbyterians by the English, and wound up in the delta country of Mississippi in the early years of the 19th century. They were farmers up to my father's generation.

It seems odd to me that my father never once mentioned the jar to me during his lifetime. Then again, knowing my carelessness, maybe it wasn't so odd. I asked my aunts and uncles about the jar, but they knew nothing of it. The records of the Midway Baptist Church, of which we were members, are quite thorough from 1808 to the present – I have gone through them carefully and there is no mention, even a veiled reference, to such an artifact. Although Baptists believe in miracles, my guess is that they would have pooh-poohed the authenticity of the jar as being too Catholic a phenomenon, like relics of saints, or a piece of the True Cross, or the Shroud of Turin.

My father's will stipulated that I was to inherit the jar and that it should be opened on the occasion of my wedding. I will be getting married, for the first time, in just over a month, on the eve of my 60th birthday. Maybe the existence of the jar is what caused me to wait so long. He never mentioned, in his will or to my mother, why, after almost 2,000 years, it was to be opened at *my* wedding. At first, just the idea of it gave me the willies; it was kind of an emotional albatross. Then I thought that maybe it was a joke, but neither my mother nor my father were inclined to make jokes or play pranks.

When my mother first handed me the jar, I felt its shape, its coolness. It literally made my hands buzz. Just holding it seemed to lift me out of my perpetual funk. I shook it gingerly, and could tell that there was still a certain amount of liquid inside. I began to cry, and handed it back to my mother, who cried also. I asked her to keep it for me, until I married. I have held it only twice since then.

That was 30 years ago. There were several times when I was on the verge of marriage, but none of those situations panned out. My mother told me that when she met you the first time, she knew that you were the right one. Last year, when we postponed our wedding, she said that she was almost beside herself.

I know that this is the first time that I have ever mentioned the jar to you. As my brothers, sisters and I myself have begun to experience our own mortality I thought it best to tell them about the jar. Naturally, they were bewildered. It is my intention to ask my mother to transport the jar to our wedding. If she puts it in her luggage that she checks through, I think it will be fine. I can't imagine that x-raying it will change it in any way, after 2,000 years. But what do I know.

It is my plan to stand up at *our* wedding feast and explain the jar. I could open it in private, but I am not embarrassed to witness in this way – despite what skeptics may think. I know, also, that you have a hard time believing in anything that smacks of the supernatural – I hope *you* will not be embarrassed.

I will open the jar, then pour the wine into two glasses and we will hold it to the light of that fading mid-May afternoon. Then we will drink it. I know that it has not turned to sludge or to acrid brown powder – it is still wine. I expect it to taste like nothing we have ever tasted before. I'm sure the skeptics would tell us to have it analyzed before we drink it. Will we experience something like what Dom Perignon tasted when he "invented" champagne? Will it have a celestial bouquet, or will we discern the dew on the grapes of a hillside in Galilee? We will not drink all of it, but let anyone else who wishes to partake of it to do so.

I hesitate to tell you about the jar, knowing your pragmatic nature, and that you yearn to believe in the existence of such things, but that they have never happened to you. But believe me. It will change everything. Yes, *we* will be changed forever. You have already prepared me for whatever alchemy the wine may work; my life was water – your love has changed it into the finest wine.

LEFT HAND